The Museum of Marriage
and other stories

Fa Laura~
All best,
MWhA 8/11/23

The Museum of Marriage

and Other Stories

C.W Smith

LITERARY PRESS
LAMAR UNIVERSITY

ISBN: 978-1-942956-98-3

Library of Congress Control Number: 2023938842
Cover Concept: Alex Green

Lamar University Literary Press
Beaumont, TX

For William and Helen, the gold standard

And for Marcia who met it

Recent Prose by Lamar University Literary Press

Robert Bonazzi, *Awakened by Surprise*
David Bowles, *Border Lore: Folktales and Legends of South Texas*
Kevin K. Casey, *Four-Peace*
Terry Dalrymple, *Love Stories (Sort of)*
Gerald Duff, *Legends of Lost Man Marsh*
Randolf Feezell, *Beyond the Fields*
Britt Haraway, *Early Men*
Michael Howarth, *Fair Weather Ninjas*
Gretchen Johnson, *The Joy of Deception*
Tom Mack & Andrew Geyer, *A Shared Voice*
Moumin Quazi, *Migratory Words*
Harold Raley, *Lost River Anthology*
Harold Raley, *Louisiana Rogue*
Jim Sanderson, *Trashy Behavior*
Jan Seale, *A Lifetime of Words*
Jan Seale, *Appearances*
Jan Seale, *Ordinary Charms*
Melvin Sterne, *The Number You Have Reached*
Melvin Sterne, *Redemption*
Melvin Sterne, *The Shoeshine Boy*
John Wegner, *Love Is Not a Dirty Word*

Acknowledgements

Some stories in this collection were previously published, and I'd like to express gratitude to the editors of the following publications for putting them into print:

Texas Bound III
The Southwest Review
descant

CONTENTS

The Balcony Scene

We were toasting marshmallows at a campfire. Earlier during a shower, we'd eaten a potluck dinner under a stone shelter built by the CCC. It had also rained a bit in the afternoon when we kids went hiking above the falls, and now from our elevated campsite, here at twilight we watched a ruddy rivulet ease over the crossing below where the lone road led to the Carlsbad highway. Archie Duncan said the crossing could flood. We weren't due to break camp until morning, and the men thought the water would recede by then.

Jack Woodley said he'd planned to leave before dawn and didn't want to be stranded. He had a meeting in the morning. It took two hours to drive home in perfect conditions, and beyond the crossing lay several miles of gravel road to the first paved highway. "We'd best head out now."

Mrs. Woodley was bent over helping her toddler, Buddy, with his roasting stick, and she swung upright to say, "Oh, Jack, don't be silly! There's plenty of time in the morning."

Jack looked annoyed to be contradicted in public by his wife. "Louise," he said, "This is not a meeting we can afford for me to miss."

"Looks like it could rise pretty fast," said Archie Duncan.

"Aw, well, that Pontiac's good as a duck. Let's go, hon."

"Jack!"

"I said let's go!"

I snuck a glance at Jeannie. She was three kids down from me prodding the flames with a coat-hanger wire, gaze fixed on the blackening orb impaled on the end. Her cheeks were flushed, maybe from the fire. Mrs. Woodley bent to blow on Buddy's flaming glob. She seemed to mull it over. To distract the younger kids from the Woodley's argument, my mother chirped about needing more marshmallows.

Finally, Jack said, "You and the kids want to stay, somebody can give you a lift tomorrow." He looked at the other adults. Jack Woodley worked for Humble, and my dad worked for Gulf, and Archie Duncan for Skelly. Our town was an overgrown constellation of company encampments built for employees during the boom back in the 1930s, and we and the Woodleys lived in them. A men's service club had organized this campout. Carl Fritz owned a dry-goods store, another fellow sold insurance, and the group included a teacher, Mr. Showalter, a bachelor who'd taught me math in the 7th grade.

I hoped someone would offer, but Mrs. Woodley said, "I'm not about to let you go by yourself."

"Okay, then. Let's get a move on." He turned toward the campsites. "Now!" he called over his shoulder. Jeannie sighed and handed her wire to Calvin Duncan. I watched her trail her parents and her brother down the hill. I was sorry to see her leave. I'd formed a new notion about her; I didn't know exactly what it was but wanted to explore it.

Jeannie: Tall, lanky, hardly-breasted yet (padded bra), no makeup or jewelry, but kitty-cat glasses and wavy blonde hair that never seemed much brushed. Mr. Woodley was a geologist, what she wanted to be. She sometimes wore dresses her mother had made. This wasn't so bizarre, then. Our mothers had gone through the Depression, so many were cottage seamstresses—my mother sewed pajamas for me, my dad, and herself. But to a typical teenage girl, homemade duds marked you as poor and peculiar. Jeannie's female peers favored big poodle skirts and saddle oxfords.

Jeannie didn't attend our football or basketball games, nor did she come to sock hops. She played violin, and it went without saying that she disdained our Elvis and the rockabillies who brayed from the studios of our radio station.

One day in ninth-grade English Miss Newman broke a nib and said the fountain pen was part of her collection. How many pens do you have? Rena Doty asked. Maybe twenty, said Miss Newman. Do you have any collections? Rena answered bunnies— not real ones, glass and pottery and wood and stuff. Anybody else have collections? Kenneth Goodrum had a bunch of fishing lures. Janet Martinez had barrettes and some brooches from her grandmother. I thought of my albums of stamps, but a newfound sense of manhood that had arrived with pubic hair made me say, because I had two, that I collected pocket knives.

Jeannie said, "I collect mnemonic devices." Snickers. What's that? someone asked. Jeanne twisted in her front row seat to peer at her classmates. "It's a made-up word or phrase to remember things, like Every Good Boy Does Fine and FACE for the notes on a musical staff. Also, like HOMES for the names of the Great Lakes. I especially like this one—Please Excuse My Dear Aunt Sally. It's how you can remember the order of operations in algebra. Parentheses, Exponents, Multiplication, Division, Addition, Subtraction."

We called her a "know-it-all" because she did know it all. Her hand shot up at the teacher's every question, and her answers brightened Miss Newman's day. But I, too, sat on the front row, and my hand usually went up. If she answered first, I'd immediately contradict her, and she never let my answer go uncontested. Sometimes Miss Newman had to stop our volleys.

Here you go: Frost's "Stopping by the Woods on a Snowy Evening." Miss Newman asked what we thought about the word "But" in "The woods are lovely, dark, and deep. But I have promises to keep." And why does he repeat "And miles to go before I sleep." Jeannie got the first nod, though my hand was aloft. She said the man was feeling very tired, so tired that maybe going to sleep in the woods would be like he says 'lovely,' even though he might die there, but that might be okay. And he says "miles to go before I sleep" twice to remind himself he has a lot more life to live before he can die.

Aw, that's nuts! I blurted out. I said it was about "duty over beauty," and instantly felt proud of that phrase. "Duty over beauty," I repeated. I said he stops "because the scene is so, you know, alluring, that he wants to really appreciate it." Jeanne tittered, no doubt because I'd said alluring. I said the poem's not about dying. It's just that "as much as he'd like to stop and smell the roses, he's got too much stuff to do."

Jeannie countered that there weren't any roses in the poem. And why is it the "darkest" night? Miss Newman broke in to ask if anyone else had thoughts. No one did. Miss Newman said the nice thing about the poem is that the ambiguity allows us to consider the different things it might mean.

Then there's the Balcony Scene. Video and streaming didn't exist, but Miss Newman owned 78 rpm records on which actors recited soliloquies from "Romeo and Juliet." She planned to read some scenes aloud, summarize others, have us read at home, and listen to the records.

And we students would read aloud, too. She looked over the classroom. Would any of you girls volunteer to play Juliet? Jeanne's hand flailed in the air. Miss Newman got at least two other contenders. Oh, well, thank you, girls! We'll have you trade off. Now how about Romeo...

Ours was a small-town school in oil, cattle, and cotton country of Southeastern New Mexico. The Catholic diocese had a K-8, but their high-schoolers had to attend here. Our chapter of The Future Farmers of America was huge. Our chapter of the National Honor Society was tiny. I did not raise my hand. Playing Romeo would be deadly to my new manly image.

She waited, tapping her desk with her capped pen.

Finally, she said, "James, how about you?"

"Uh, mm," I grunted. I took a quick glance at Jeannie whose evil grin said, I dare you. I'll be ten times better.

Miss Newman took advantage of my waffling. "Good. Well, I want the two of you to study the famous 'balcony scene' and prepare a reading for the class."

"Together?"

"Certainly, that'd be most beneficial and efficient. Maybe you could meet during study hall if not at home."

It was the worst homework assignment I'd ever gotten. I don't think Jeannie was expecting it, either. Her knees jittered up and down, and she sent all her fingers through her hair. I stared at Miss Newman. Surely, she could guess how awkward this would be for us.

Shortly after, we had one session during study hall. We were reading from tattered paperbacks, and I'd been lucky to get one used by a very dutiful reader—much helpful marginalia and, a bonus, answers to Mr. Simpson's pop history quizzes inside the back cover.

Jeannie had chosen a far corner of the cafeteria away from other students. Romeo's long monologue opens the scene, but I insisted that we start with Juliet's first lines. She agreed begrudgingly.

Jeannie: " O Romeo, Romeo! wherefore art thou Romeo! Deny thy—"

Me: "I'm right here, dummy. Look up."

She did look up. To glare. "In the first place, it doesn't mean where are you. It means why are you Romeo, why are you a Montague."

I knew that, as it was scribbled in the margin. Okay, I said. "Go again."

Jeannie: " O Romeo, Romeo! wherefore art thou Romeo! Deny thy—"

Me: "Why am I Romeo? Gee, it's what my parents named me."

She slammed her book shut. She was trembling, near tears. "You're not even going to try, are you!"

She leapt up, scattering papers then furiously scooping them up along with a tube of Chapstick and a half-eaten Snickers she'd meticulously closed the wrapper over. She threw them into a baggy floral purse that looked like one my granny might tote. She left her opened bottle of Coke behind. I'd swigged it half down before realizing her lips had touched it.

The next day Miss Newman held me after class. "I knew there was friction, but I thought you two could put it aside. Jeannie wants to give up the role unless she has a different Romeo. What do you think?"

"Jeannie wants a different Romeo?" I didn't know why, but this bothered me.

"Or else she wants you to take it seriously."

Even I could see the justice of the reprimand. "Okay," I said. "I can do that."

"You might start by apologizing to her."

Most of the kids had never been here. To me, the place was magical. The USDA's recreation area at Sitting Bull Falls in the Lincoln National Forest in the high New Mexican desert offered my only encounter with spring-fed creeks that meandered through barren hills and engendered a lush narrow valley that might look like Kelly-colored rick-rack from the air. The streams converged and tumbled over boulders up in the canyons, creating clear pools with stone bottoms, feeding cottonwoods and agaritas with their red berries that my mother turned into jelly, aspens even, madrone trees that shed pages of sepia bark, flowering yucca, so-called century plants, and shoulder-high native grasses.

From the campsites, a path led to the base of the falls that plunged off the cliffs in stages, the water pooling for wading and swimming. Hidden behind the falls was a cave reached by climbing crude, slippery stone steps aside a sheet of water, and I planned to lead the others there and tell probably more than I knew about it.

The adults had charged me with shepherding the "little kids" who'd wheedled their way onto the roster. I loaded my Boy Scout's knapsack with my flashlight, a box of Cheezits, and a can of Vienna sausages. I had an aluminum canteen in a canvas holster that fixed to my belt. I'd bought it at a military surplus store, and I filled it with grape Kool-Aid. I owned a hunting knife in a leather sheath. Fully loaded, I fairly bristled with preparedness.

Aside from a half dozen teens, there were grammar-school twerps, three boys and one of their sisters. I had them circle up, and, resting my palm on the butt of my hunting knife, I told them that the trail ahead held many dangers. You, Jack Fritz, could fall off a cliff or get bitten by rattlers or Gila monsters or mountain lions or tarantulas, and if you, Clarence, hope to have you and your sister Janice come back in one piece, then you'd best keep me in sight. If I can't see you, I'll call you with a secret whistle (here, I jammed two fingers in my mouth and blew three shrill notes), but if you ever tell anybody what it is, I will have to terminate you.

What's terminate?

That's for me to know and you to find out.

What's a Gila monster?

It's a giant lizard big as a dog with poisonous fangs like a rattlesnake.

We struck off from the campsites as a group, but soon Calvin Duncan steered Julie Watson ahead because they wanted to be alone, leaving Ricky Barber and Lucille Page, along with Jeannie and the four twerps, traipsing behind me. We scrambled up a stony incline beside the plummeting columns whose fluted skirt kicked up dazzling mists that conjured rainbows. Just at the edge of the water's flank, the path ducked behind the spuming sheets and became wet stairsteps. I mounted myself beside the path against the stone wall to give my wards a hand to secure them. I took Jeannie's with an air of a professional tour guide performing an obligatory duty. She didn't look at me. Her fingers were warm cupped in my palm, and I let them go a nanosecond before it was truly safe.

The cave entrance was big as a classroom. The natural lighting was sufficient, but for effect I used my flashlight as a pointer. A firepit held chunks of charred wood, an empty can of pork and beans, and a red wrapper from a pack of Pall Malls. If you ignored the signs of contemporary visitors, it was easy to imagine this as a sanctuary for ancient peoples. Recent natives had carved modern pictographs into the walls. Kilroy was here. Wildcats. BJ + NS inside a heart.

"How come it's called Sitting Bull Falls?" asked Clarence. "Did an Indian name it?"

I said it was probably named after chief Sitting Bull.

"But he wouldn't have come here personally," declared Jeannie. "He was a Lakota Sioux Indian. I think they stayed mostly up in North and South Dakota."

She'd apparently read up on it.

Two twerps were larking about where the back wall narrowed to a dark tunnel. My dad and I had once gone a few yards into it with a flashlight until it closed to a crawl space neither of us wanted to negotiate.

Jeannie said, "You kids be careful! It's slippery back there." Was she was helping me or competing?

"Where's that go, anyway?" asked Jack.

I told them that my dad and I had explored it. "We went a couple miles. Then we came to this big room way down there. We found a skeleton! A skeleton in a coat of armor! I'm pretty sure he was one of Coronado's con-kiss-tah-doors."

"Aw, really?" asked Clarence's sister, Janice.

Jeannie was smirking.

"Yeah, really! And there were doubloons scattered right—"

"What're those?"

"Spanish gold coins. Hundreds of them."

Jeannie laughed.

"Yeah, and we got pretty excited. I bent over to pick up one, but all of a sudden"—(pause for dramatic effect)—"one of those big icicle things that hang from the ceiling like daggers or swords, you know, like at Carlsbad Caverns, it fell right by us with a giant crash! If I'd bent over farther to pick one of those doubloons, that stalagmite would've stabbed me right in my back!"

"Really?"

"Really. And then from way down in the cave came this voice, really quivery and trembly like an ancient ghost, and it was moaning, 'Noo nooo nooo.' Just then my flashlight went out! And my dad said we better skedaddle and not take anything because whatever is down there—" I jabbed a finger at the darkness behind us. "Whatever the heck it is just might try to stop us from leaving."

"Wow!" said Clarence.

Ricky and Lucille were laughing. Jeannie smiled. "James means stalaCtite," she said to them all. "Not stalaGmite. You can remember the difference with the C for 'ceiling' or the G for 'ground.'"

Moments later, I stood at the mouth of the cave next to the dazzling skein of water, feeling it mist my face. The waterfall wall provoked a dreamy, hypnotic state, as if I were an Apache.

Jeannie eased beside me. I steeled myself.

"My daddy gave me stuff to read about this area." She slid her hands into the mist and turned them over and over, her skin glistening. She had long fingers, and I wondered if she played piano, too. "It's hard to imagine now because it's so dry and hilly, but like 250 million years ago in the Permian period, this was under a sea. It was called the Great Capital Barrier Reef, I think."

"How do they know that?"

"When they drill down to get a core sample, they find fossilized marine creatures that died on the ocean floor and got buried in the sediment."

"Huh! Well, I like it better this way."

"Yeah, me too!" She turned her palms up like cups. "It's really special. Thanks for bringing us here."

James the Tour Guide answered, "You're very welcome." And then I recalled I still hadn't apologized for acting up in study hall. I told myself that being courteous was the same as, or at least as good as, an apology.

In the waning twilight, you couldn't quite gauge how far up the road the water had inched, but its steady course through the gulleys made glimmering highlights on the surface.

"As for that Puny-ack being good as a duck, that's bull hockey," said Archie Duncan.

"Well, let's don't go wishing him bad luck," said Junior Fretz.

They traded stories about having their cars or homes flooded. One fellow I didn't know bragged that he'd crossed swollen creeks like that near his hunting lease dozens of times—you just have to bear down and gun it, he said. Mr. Showalter said he got swept clean off his feet while wading across a flooded river and would've drowned if he hadn't smacked against a tree and climbed it. Was it too risky to chance going with the family in the car? I looked down the hill for Jeannie. I wondered if she was scared.

The insurance agent said, "Seeing he's made up his mind, least we can do is help get him off."

At the Woodley's campsite, he and two other fellows had uprooted the tent stakes and laid the canvas flat. He seemed jittery, scattered, stepping off this way and that, then stopping abruptly as if suddenly recalling something. He told his helpers to fold the damn thing up any which way to stuff it into his trunk, and he'd redo it later. Mrs. Woodley was putting tin camp plates into a cardboard box. Jeannie was loading their green Coleman cooler with a milk jug and plastic food containers. Little Buddy kept interrupting their work by whining and wanting to wander off.

"Can I help?" I asked.

Mrs. Woodley said, "Why, thank you, James! You and Jeannie can take the cook pot and go get water to douse that fire. And for God's sake, take Buddy with you!"

I could've offered to put the fire out later, but I had unfinished business with Jeannie.

On our earlier excursion up in the canyon, Ricky and Lucille scrambled ahead to find Calvin and Julie and spoil their fun. It was slow-going over slick boulders and loose scree, and I had to keep an eye on the twerps. There wasn't a trail, really—you worked your way along the creek to keep from getting lost. Clarence jammed his foot in a crevasse, and when he pulled his foot free, the shoe stayed stuck, so we stopped to extract it. Janice slipped and scraped her knee, so Jeannie dipped her own handkerchief into the creek to wipe the dirt and blood.

"What about a Band-aid?" Janice whined. "Don't I have to have a Band-aid?"

"We don't have any," I said. A minor dereliction of my duty. Jeannie tied her hanky around the knee and said that would be as good.

Then the Fritz brothers ran after a rabbit, and I whistled but they either didn't hear or plain ignored me, so I chased them down and chastised them. Clarence wanted to climb a cottonwood. Jack Duncan tried drinking from a pool but fell on his face into the water. After we'd persuaded him that he'd dry off as we hiked, Jeannie murmured this aside to me: "Gosh! These kids are a lot of trouble!"

And I replied, "You said it!" Suddenly I felt like an adult, with Jeannie and I in a parental partnership, responsible but also to be held accountable. I wondered if she felt it, too.

A sudden shower sent us scurrying under an overhang, hunkered, my bare left arm smashed against Jeannie's bare right arm, the kids squirming and wriggly, Janice cozy in Jeannie's lap. I dug the Cheezits from my knapsack and passed the box around. I opened the Vienna sausages, saw one apiece. I impaled each on the point of my hunting knife to serve them, but Janice dropped hers in the dirt and started whimpering. I gave her the last one. Then I plucked the dirty one off the ground, rinsed it with Kool-Aid, and swallowed it whole.

"Yuck!" said Janice.

"Double yuck!" laughed Jeannie.

I passed the canteen, starting with Jeannie because I guessed she wouldn't want to drink after the rest of us. When Janice took a big slug, half went down her neck, and she whined that it felt all sticky. When the boys had had their turn, I pointed to a crease on the belly of the canteen.

"See that? This canteen belonged to a Marine, and a Japanese sniper shot at him but only grazed the canteen right here."

Twerp eyes got all wide. Jeannie said, pointing to the holster, "But wouldn't the bullet have to go through that cover first?"

"Yeah, yeah. Okay. That is a replacement that Marine got because the bullet ruined the original."

"Clever fellow," said Jeannie.

The rain stopped, and we untangled and set off. Shortly after, Clarence and Janice got away from us, and Jeannie and I separated to find them. I took a lower track. Jeannie climbed to the top of a big boulder and called for them. Below, I looked up. She'd hooded her eyes from the sun, but her soft chin and generous mouth were bright in the light, full lips the color of watermelon. Now I noticed that in her side-zip jeans her hips seemed fuller than I'd thought. I considered those Cinderella makeovers—there was plenty of good material here to work with.

I called up to her. "But, soft! What light through yonder window breaks? It is the east, and Juliet is the sun."

Startled, she cocked her head down. And blushed.

"Sorry," I said. "I don't have any more memorized."

She grinned. "Oh, Romeo!" She shook her head in mock dismay. "Thou art incorrigible."

There! I thought. Now I've apologized.

Later, as we came out of the canyon near the trail to the shelters, the twerps bolted with an air of gleefully flouting our authority. Just before we reached the swimming pool where adults were lounging in camp chairs, Jeannie stopped abruptly.

"James. I have to ask you something."

"Okay."

She was looking at her sneakers. "My mom wants to know if you'll go to the Sadie Hawkins Day dance."

I was baffled. Inspired by a tradition in the comic strip "L'il Abner," once a year the girls got to ask the boys out.

"Can't your mom get your dad to take her?"

"Don't be stupid!" After a beat, she added, "She thinks I don't have enough friends."

I was slow to get it because it was so unexpected. She took my hesitation for rejection, and said, "Jeez. Never mind! If it's okay I'll just tell her you said yes then you can be sick or something."

She strode down the trail in a huff. I didn't know what to think but felt I'd not been given a chance to answer. I caught up to her, pinched her blouse sleeve to stop her.

"Okay. I mean it's okay to tell her I said yes."

But I didn't know if I meant yes to the date or yes to the plan to fake it for her mom.

****

I was puzzled but oddly pleased. Though the invitation had come via her mother, Jeannie could've said, "Oh, Mom, not him!" Or just told her mother I'd said no or I was busy, then never mention it to me.

She liked me? I thought she hated me, that I annoyed her. And what did I really feel? When I'd heard she'd be coming on the campout, I moaned aloud but my pulse beat a bit faster to imagine the tiffs and parrying we could do as unpleasant entertainment.

At that age, I was ignorant of the "love/hate" cliche. The couple clashes on that first cute meet; their mutual disdain keeps the story rolling until, say, one wounds the other too deeply. That provokes surrender in one and remorse in the other, then the spark between them arcs into the electric agreement that makes magnets. But I had no template for what was passing between us then. My feelings were singular, unique in human history, my confusion a forest I was lost in without the compass of that precedent.

I carried the cook pot to the community spigot while she toted her three-year-old brother V-ed on her hip. I snuck sidelong glances at her profile to try to clarify my feelings, but they were a morass of irresistible but alarming confusion. I wasn't used to realizing I might be a girl's preference, especially one who supposedly detested me.

The water spigot was a good fifty yards away along a sandy path. Buddy was more content now to be in his sister's arms. Jeannie seemed closed off, frowning at the path before our feet.

I wanted to say I wish you could stay but instead said, "Don't worry. Your dad's a real good driver. It'll be okay."

She sighed. "He gets ideas in his head that he has to do something or that something has to happen and nobody not even my mother can make a dent in it."

"He's stubborn?"

"More than that. I don't even know what to call it."

I almost said, Well, that's a first.

"Do you think they'd let you stay with somebody and come home tomorrow?" I would've even offered to practice our balcony scene if we'd had the text.

She sighed. "No. My mom needs me."

A couple of men parked just off the road where it disappeared into the water. When they switched their headlights on, the rays struck debris protruding from the surface as it floated downstream. There was no gauge, so the men took guesses as to how deep it was, but nobody could say for sure. It still might be easily passable. Earlier the sky had been clear, but a sodden overcast had snuck in, and when you looked to the crossing's far side, a gray miasma hid the road. The headlights brightened the opaque skein without penetrating it. What they knew for sure, they agreed, was that it was best to go as soon as possible.

I watched Jack Woodley wave his wife into the Pontiac's passenger side with shooing hand swipes. Jeannie was trying to corral her little brother while looping a knapsack strap over her shoulder. I wondered what I'd do in his place, what I might do in the future as a husband, father, provider. Earlier Jack had said that this meeting he had to make tomorrow morning was important. Maybe I would chance it, maybe not. I'd be afraid I'd regret missing the meeting if it was important, and maybe I'd feel that the manly thing was to take risks to get rewards, not shrink back.

My dad and four other men walked to the water's edge. I tried to measure my own apprehension against what I saw in the grown men. What was I supposed to be feeling? How should I act? Last night the men went down to the crossing away from the women and children to drink beer and smoke cigars (I was apparently old enough to audit), and they traded war stories, which were thrilling to me. Mr. Showalter said he'd clambered down a cargo net off Sicily and waded onshore, got shot at and scared spitless but otherwise crept up the whole damn boot of Italy without mishap except for a Jeep wreck that gave him a concussion. Archie Duncan was a Marine radioman. A sniper at Tarawa had shot off his helmet, but his squad's flamer set the sniper's tree afire, and they watched while he fell like a flaming comet fifty feet to the jungle floor. Jack Woodley was on a destroyer's ack-ack crew, and they'd blown a dozen kamikaze Zeroes to smithereens before they could slam into their ship, and Junior Fretz was a B-24 nose-gunner who flew missions over Germany. I knew my Dad was embarrassed by having spent the war working in the oil fields, but I believed he would've been as brave as the rest of them. I kept thinking, how would I have acted? Would I have the courage? Would I be man enough?

Now, Archie Duncan was frowning, hands chocked on his hips, and my Dad was looking upstream while Mr. Showalter was apparently telling a joke to the fellow who'd bragged about his derring-do at the creek crossings, and then they were both laughing. It didn't seem they were worried, and I thought my worry was childish, maybe, not manly.

The Woodleys closed their doors. He started his engine, and the car eased down toward the waterline. I was standing by my dad at the water's foaming edge, and my mother came up and said, "Rob, I can't watch this," and walked away. Two other women with children led them off, too. I was proud to be among the men.

When his front tires touched the water, the red brake lights flared up then off. We stared intently at the doors and wheels to judge the water's depth. We watched the tires go hub-cap deep. Earlier, Junior Fretz said it was best to cross fast so the water wouldn't swamp the engine and that a heavy car's momentum would carry it on. But someone else said the faster you drove, the bigger wave you'd make would stall you out.

Jack Woodley revved the Pontiac's engine, but at midstream, the car was bull-dozing a billow of flood water. The water lapped against the flanks, surged over the back bumper, and when it swallowed the tailpipe, the engine died.

Then the car lifted slightly. The rear wheels slid downstream, and the car cocked at an angle. We heard Mrs. Woodley screaming.

"Aw, Christ!" groaned Archie Duncan.

The car rocked and floated away, and soon it slid invisible beyond the car lights. Something chrome glinted back from the dark, as if the car had hung up on a tree or a boulder. Mrs. Woodley was still screaming. Then the men's flashlights together were strong enough to show the driver's door cocked open and Jack Woodley up to his neck in water. He was clinging to the doorframe. He hollered for help.

Archie Duncan had rappelling rope in his trunk, and he ran and retrieved it. When he was holding it before the others, seemingly at a loss, my Dad took it. "Here, hold this!" He handed Mr. Showalter an end of a rope, then he tied the other to his waist.

He waded into the water. I wanted to yell, "Wait!" Archie Duncan and Mr. Showalter looped their end around their arms to brace against the current, then they edged in up to their shins to give my dad more slack. The water rose to his waist as he slogged downstream toward the sinking car, and when he started swimming, I knew he'd been shoved off his feet. Junior Fretz tied another rope to himself, anchored an end to a car bumper, then he used the rope attached to my dad as a guide and went in after him.

The men yelled back and forth across the darkness, and soon I saw Mrs. Woodley and Junior Fretz struggling against the current with each tied to a rope. Archie Duncan and Mr. Showalter tugged them through the rushing water, and I leapt to take a hank of the rope between my hands to help. I knew then that my dad had untied himself to hook up Mrs. Woodley. He was untethered, so would he need rescue? Had he been carried away?

While Mrs. Woodley sobbed in the arms of another woman, I asked Junior Fretz, "Is my dad okay?" He was too intent on another go to hear me. Moments later, Jeannie was brought back. I wanted to talk to her, but she was too distraught, and they laid her covered in a back seat and elevated her feet.

We watched Junior Fretz's back as he plunged into the waves, and the current carried him into the darkness. Many moments later, our flashlights caught two heads bobbing inside the opened front door. Then their faces turned to us—Junior had tied himself and Mr. Woodley to the ropes. Archie Duncan, Mr. Showalter, and I tugged against the current with all our strength to pull them to safety.

When the two stood safe on the road, Jack Woodley bent with palms on his thighs, gasped, and puked.

"Where's my dad?!" I yelled. "Did you leave him there?"

Mrs. Woodley hurled herself at him. "Buddy! Didn't you get Buddy?!" She kept shoving his chest. "Where's Buddy!"

"Rob's looking for him," said Junior Fretz. As he was heading back into the rushing stream, he said, "Don't worry, Jimmy. I won't come back without him."

The rain started up again, and our flashlights wouldn't penetrate the dark curtain beyond the headlights. Then I could hear my dad yelling to pull, then we saw him and Junior Fretz clutching the ends of the ropes, and within minutes they were back with us. I took three steps and grabbed ahold of him, had to bite my lip to keep from sobbing out loud.

"Where's Buddy?" pleaded Mrs. Woodley.

My dad and Junior Fretz exchanged a look. My dad said, "He wasn't in the car, Louise. I'm sorry."

For hours we scoured the camp side of the crossing, pointing our flashlights into every crevice, every slough and dip, and, hours later, when the water went down, we slogged along the other bank. Jack Woodley huddled under a blanket drinking coffee in someone's car, afraid to face us, I thought. A woman I didn't know gave Jeannie a tranquilizer and she stayed dazed in the car. Louise Woodley hiked up along the banks, shivering in wet clothes, frantically calling for the boy until two women made her sit by a campfire covered with a poncho.

I stuck close to my dad. If he did anything like that again, I had to be there to help him. I got reflected glory, too, because as we searched, people murmured Thanks to you, really heroic and the like, and my dad shrugged and said, Well, we all did what anybody would. Just after dawn, Mimi Fretz found Buddy's body far downstream from the crossing. He was nested in the branches of a big mesquite, where the flood had dropped him like flotsam.

Jeannie missed two days of class. Some kids at school said Jeannie's dad had been a moron to try the crossing just because he had a golf date with men he wanted to suck up to for a business deal, and his little boy had died because of it. I took up the attitude, carried it home, and aired it out in front of my mother. She said, "James, you've got no idea what it means to be responsible for the welfare of others. The Woodleys were having serious money trouble. It's not your business to know, but I can tell you Jack's company has laid off his entire department just so they won't have to cover their health insurance and retirement benefits, and they'll use contractors for the work. Jack was doing what he felt he had to do, and you're not in any position to criticize."

During Jeannie's absence, I wanted to call her home, but I'd had no experience consoling survivors, and it scared me. Meanwhile, Miss Newman assigned me another Juliet, a girl I remembered from the fifth grade because she'd sucked hard candy on the sly nonstop and tossed the wrappers in the book hold beneath her seat.

When Jeannie came back to school, her presence electrified us. She'd suffered a great loss but also a great shame, so it was as if she glowed from swallowing plutonium. I expected her to behave as if everything were normal and so obligate us to deny her condition and predicament. While we studied Emerson's "Concord Hymn," she sat mute and never raised her hand. I wanted to tell her I felt sorry for her. As I considered what to say, I imagined myself as the Ambassador from the Family of Heroes. I'd step down from my cloud to offer a hand of compassion and forgiveness to this poor wretch from the Family of Unfortunates. I'd be magnanimous. I'd be roundly congratulated for it.

But the distance seemed enormous. I knew the Sadie Hawkins Dance was a burst bubble, and the fragile thing we'd engendered briefly had been swept aside by what our fathers had done and how our families would live with it.

The Museum of Marriage

The Bundlelays are a big mystery to me. They're that two-story Victorian with the wrap-around porch and the ginger-bread molding down on the corner. The house anchors our block. It makes a stately impression, but it would make a better one if they refurbished it like the redone "grandma houses" on gentrified blocks close by.

We're talking total gut redo—they're still using window units and there's only one full bath upstairs and a half down and the fixtures are pretty much the originals installed in the late teens. Their son wanted them to sell, and so behind their backs he roped me into agreeing to list it before I knew what was up. The elder Mr. Bundlelay had "a little stroke" and Mrs. B was sleeping at his hospital room in a chair, so the son gave me a tour. He said they were moving to a condo near him in Las Colinas so that his wife and their grown daughter could look after them.

I've specialized in urban properties ever since divorcing a guy I caught selling my unlaundered underwear over the internet. Actually, that was among the least of our problems, but telling people this distracts them from a truly embarrassing discussion of our differences. We were living in a brand-new "Coon-ass Gothic" monster with 4500 square feet, way too much of which was wasted space in "cathedral" ceilings unless you convert it into an aviary. From the front it looked just like Darlie Routier's house in Mesquite, and that like scared me sometimes. Justin grew up on the outskirts of San Antonio and went to college on the fringe of Dallas, so our house was way out in the burbs. When we split up, I went zoom! right into the city looking for a real-life neighborhood that hadn't been ethnically cleansed and bought my house here on Vanderbilt. It took three years to strip it out, replumb, rewire and reroof, install central heat and air and refinish the floors (wonderful oak hiding under wall-to-wall for thirty years). Painted every square inch inside and out. Meanwhile I studied for my broker's license and I was a manager at Kroger's. My house isn't like the Bundlelays'—it's a prairie-style bungalow, built in '33 as a 2/1, and I added a big bath and a big family room with a fireplace at the back, though I'm the only family right now, if you don't count Kevin.

The Bundlelays are in their 90s, and I admit I've lusted for that house. When their son called, I toyed with selling this one, rolling up my sleeves and spending a ton of money, winding up with a show-case down there. Put it on the spring homes tour, get featured in magazines. (I admit to premature thoughts too about Kevin's busi-ness—he's a free-lance photographer, and that Bundlelay house has an unfinished third-story space with dormer windows.)

Four bedrooms up, and downstairs are your dining room, parlor, living and breakfast rooms, big kitchen. Ten-foot ceilings. It has wonderful features you don't find any more—fan light with beveled glass above the entrance door, crown molding, Rookwood tile around the fireplace, and diamond glass doorknobs. But the Bundlelays have been there sixty years, and for the last twenty they've been short the bustle and the bucks to keep it up. The foun-dation needs a $10K redo, then because of that you'd have to strip the walls of that old plastered lathe and Sheetrock them, but that would rid you of that ancient cheesy wallpaper. You'd start below and not stop until you were on the chimney where a couple bricks are missing and there's no bird or cinder guard. You'd be a month clearing out their things. One bedroom has towers of National Geographics going back to the 1940s. Nobody's lived on the second floor in five years—that's sad—and the son said that they spend the better part of an afternoon hoisting one another up the stairs to bathe in the only tub. He said that they joked that it's just like going to the swimming hole in their younger days. They sleep in the parlor now.

I told him that in the current market the house might bring $500K at the very most because a buyer would have to plunk down another hundred, a good $50K in the kitchen alone and another $50K for a master bath. Our inner-city property is appreciating, but "as is" can be tough to sell.

I'm sitting in my porch swing a few evenings later toking on a glass of white wine when the Bundlelays come up the street. When I see them, this realization hits me: they've been married over 60 years! That's amazing! My biopop did an DB Cooper before I could recognize him and I have to take a snapshot's word for what he looked like. I had two stepfathers – one on the record and one off. My Mom never married the second one, Frank, out of fear that marriage itself was fatal to the state of matrimony. They broke up anyway, which was a shame, because I really liked him. We still exchange Christmas cards. My Mom said, "I like being married but I just get to where I can't stand all the crap." Frank took that day-tripper bus to Bossier City weekly to hit the casinos, and I guess that's what she meant by "crap." They argued like a lot about money. Tim—my official stepfather—griped that my Mom smoked and drank too much (which she does), and when he started getting in her face to get reborn, that was the end. He did get me reborn when I was twelve, but I up and died again when I hit high school and hung out with kids who did coke and X and spent their weekends moshing in Deep Ellum. I tossed out my virginity like it was an old t-shirt I got at Disneyland when I was ten. I had a line of boyfriends who each taught me something. (But, oh, will I ever learn?) Matt believed I was more selfish than I really was, and so I learned that I was less selfish than I thought; Chris and I both believed I was more daring than I turned out to be; with Damon I learned that I always want to be the boss but I also need someone to keep me from doing that. Justin—my personal underwear broker—claimed we were "partners," but it took a while to see not equal partners. He was the silent partner; I was the working partner. He believed in mutual unilateral decision-making. We'd come home from work and eat the meal I'd stopped at Whole Foods to get for us, and then next thing I knew he'd be like standing at the front door in gym clothes, and if I caught him before he left, I'd ask, "Where you going?" "Shoot some hoops," he'd say. He'd play with his old frat brothers for a few hours then go to a bar and he wouldn't be home until midnight. All this and not word one about his plans. Or asking if I minded. I'd say, "But what if I have plans?" "Fine," he'd say. "Plans for both of us, I mean." "Well, you shoulda told me," he'd say. So, one night just as he's about to waltz wordless out the door, I say, "Oh, hey, mind dropping me off at the airport?" He goes—"The airport?" "Yeah," I say. He shrugs like that's fine but his mind's all twisty with it, shows up on his forehead like the back of a linen skirt after a day on a bus. I grab an empty suitcase, and on the way, I jabber about work and never say diddly squat about this supposed trip, so finally he says, "Where you going?" And I say, "London." He goes—"London?" He's all puzzled and hurt. I assign him household chores, like I'll be over there a good six months. He's weirded out completely but he can't show it. He pulls to the Departures curb, I get out and go "see ya!" and stroll into the terminal.

I took a cab home. He was watching tiny horse-like animals cavort halfway around the globe on ESPN2. He was surprised to see me. I'd hoped to teach him a lesson, and I could see him massaging it, but truth is he wasn't near enough disturbed by it, and that's why I say that his "panties 'r us" enterprise was not our biggest problem. I got Kevin after reading The Rules from Ellen and Sherrie, but maybe you'd call that ex post facto. The rule I was following when we met was "Show up to parties, dances and social events even if you do not feel like it," because a girl friend had begged me to go with her to a Yanni concert, and, believe me, I did not feel like it! But I'd pretty well lost faith in whatever wisdom I'd accumulated in three decades and was willing to listen to about anybody. I mean, who really knows what hooks people up, what keeps them there.

Right now, I'm in flagrant violation of their rule that says you don't date a man for more than two years—he either proposes or you say adios! I'm working up to emailing their web site about it. Anyway, the Bundlelays. They've walked in the neighborhood every evening since I moved here except when one is sick, and this was the first I'd seen them since his trip to the hospital. When they got to my front walk, I'd go down and chat about the house. They were about five doors away, though, so I wondered if I'd still be awake by then. They take their walks one step at a time. After each foot they've slid forward they seem to stop to discuss whether to suck it up and try another. But they are like really cute. From a distance they look something like a couple in a sack race; between them they've only got about two good legs. I believe she's had one knee replaced but the other's always acting up, and his arthritic hip has gone so rusty he can't walk without a cane. They totter along arm-in-arm and butted up against one another for support, leaning in like an A so that they're almost head-to-head, and although he's taller, he's been bending for six decades, and she's been stretching up, so that from a distance they're like equal tall. Push-Me-Pull-You.

They're cheek-to-cheek partly because he's half blind and she's half deaf. She's his eyes and he's her ears. He has to wear those wraparound shades, and she's got aids in both ears but the batteries always seem to be dead so they act like ear plugs. He's had a couple by-passes patched into his system and I think she's running on someone else's liver, but I could be wrong. Neither has a gall bladder. I got all this from the son, who's not exactly in the prime of youth (he has two grandchildren and looks like a cardiac cowboy).

Mrs. B's hands curl into clusters of knobby knuckles, and she can't handle utensils, so Mr. B cuts her food up—I saw this myself at our last block party—though since he can't see it very well, she has to direct him. She hollered, "Hon, it's a weenie!" and he went to work on it with a plastic fork and knife while she guided his wrist like a nuclear lab technician. Son says Mr. B has to help Mrs. B do her buttons and zippers. She can't bend enough to put on socks, but she wears slip-on shoes. Because she's deaf she talks real loud and I guess wanting to be polite he shouts too even when he's not addressing her.

They've stopped to talk with Gloria Something. Drives a red Escort, cocktail waitress. Her duplex was a single until the '60s, and she's at the end of her walk watering a plastic pot of petunias with a hose. People joke that Mr. B's "the mayor of Vanderbilt Street" because he won't let you pass without snaring you into a gabfest. He's a storehouse of "Hee Haw" openers—"You workin hard or hardly workin?" and "You walkin that dog or is he walkin you?" Except when it floods, we're always short on rain, so it's a good bet wet or dry weather will make the cut. Right now, I bet he's saying "Hot enough for you?" because it's warm for September, and I see Mrs. B oscillate her smile from one to the other like an old-timey fan—blissfully deaf, I guess—and it seems a marvel that she could listen to that blather for six decades (or until her hearing went) and not shoot herself. Or him. Now I am pretty much a people person—you don't work in real estate if you don't enjoy yakking to near-strangers half the day long—but if I were Mrs. B it might rub me raw that I can't slip through the daylight world now and then incognito under a head scarf that hides my unwashed hair. Sure as you try to stay invisible there's Mr. B dragging you by the elbow across a parking lot to shout Howdy to folks who happen to be driving the same make and color car you are.

But, sure, must be things about her that piss him off, as well. Maybe on a festive occasion when Mr. B smokes a semi-annual cigar on the porch, she'll go out and stand downwind of it to whine Pee-Yew!! and bat the air and carry on enough to like completely spoil whatever pleasure he's having.

That gets me thinking. Has anybody asked them for the secret of their marital success? I can picture their golden a decade back, a family party and a toast by that son. They'd have been milked of their wisdom earlier, and so the secret would be included in the toast. They say they owe it all to... what? Pot roast every Sunday? Fabulous bj's? If we get cozy because I'm their realtor, I can take Mrs. B for lunch at the S & S Tea Room and ask her advice about Kevin, think I've even got the hat for it. Sure, she's like old enough to be my great-grandmother and she might not get it (or hear it!) if I tell her Kevin used to be AC/DC (not that he was—but you can't be certain, right?), but you know she's got a Truth socked away that transcends generations. Better advice from her than from those geeks on Sally Jesse or Ricki Lake.

Fifty yards and closing. That's submarine talk, learned it from Justin, big Tom Clancy fan. He would read a Clancy novel even if it were only about a giant screwdriver, not an unlikely possibility, I bet. (Well, okay, a giant electric screwdriver.) Mr. B has on his geezer-glasses and this big fringed sombrero such as you get as a souvenir on a Caribbean cruise when you weigh anchor in PR—both the Bs got basal cells whacked off their noggins and he's got a pock on his nose—scuffed opera slippers without socks (Eww, Mr. B! Those ankles!), khaki pants (sometimes he wears seersucker shorts with black wing-tips and black nylon dress socks pulled like about to his knees), a short-sleeve sport shirt with a pattern I can't make out from here, and I'm presuming beneath it an undershirt with shoulder straps like old men wear even in the shower, I guess.

31

She's wearing polyester pants in an apricot hue, a white long-sleeved blouse tucked into the waistband, a string of colored beads, and a less flamboyant version of his hat. Her plastic glasses have lenses big as headlights and the curvy ear pieces attach at the bottoms. I doubt either has purchased a single garment since 1975.

I don't mean to sound snotty. They're very dear. I wish they'd been my parents and I'd spent my childhood there with my growth marked on the door each birthday instead of in a string of apartments that looked the same in different cities, apartments in land-locked states with tropical names: Palm Breeze, Enchanted Isle. (Of course, if your family has money like Justin's, then you live in a brand-new treeless suburb with a good olde English name like Village Oaks Estates or Sherwood Forest Oaks or Oakety-Oak Oaks.)

"Hi!" I holler when I saunter down to intercept them. "I don't know if you remember, but we met at last year's block party? Jennifer Walden?"

I stick my hand between them, and Mrs. B gives it a soft massage then passes it to Mr. B. He's not like completely blind. He has one of those Rotarian walnut-cracker grips, but I was captain of my volleyball team in high school and I'm up to it.

"Yes, yes!" he yells at me. "Mother was just telling me about you. Hot enough for you?"

"I'll say! We sure could stand some rain."

Mrs. B is giving me like this beatific smile but her eyes are vacant, and I swear she can't hear a word I say. Lunch would be a trial, that's for sure.

Mr. B surprises me by saying, "Philip says you'd like to sell our house."

It seems a friendly offering but the phrasing is a little pointed. I smile and say, "He asked me to check the market, you know, similar listings and such. Nothing official. I hope that's okay with you." Mrs. B says, "He's always been the sweetest boy. We hate to say no to him."

Her batteries must be working. To defend myself I say, "He told me you were moving to Las Colinas to be closer to him."

"Oh, we know he wants us to!" says Mrs. B. She's clutching Mr. B's right bicep with both hands as if it were a fireman's pole. "I'm afraid he worries far too much about us. He's very sweet that way."

"Couldn't stand it out there for a minute!" hollers Mr. B. The pattern on Mr. B's shirt turns out to be ranks of pointers with a paw lifted. "It's like the moon!"

"Traffic," puts in Mrs. B as explanation.

Mr. B says, "Nope! We'll be right here I reckon until the place falls down around our ears."

"We're used to it, you see." Mrs. B pats Mr. B's forearm to punctuate this.

We jaw a bit, then Mrs. B says, "Hon, we best be turning around, this is about as far as I can go," though I wonder if she really means this is as far as I think you ought to go. Thing is, you see, so many stories about Wonderful Lasting Marriages seem to be built on the wife's unheralded sacrifices.

I need to let Philip know what they said. I am disappointed— not about losing a chance to sell the house but to buy it. My investment as a realtor hasn't amounted to more than a few hours on my laptop comping recent sales and taking the tour (which I'd have paid for!).

The thought comes before I can squelch it that they won't last another five years, and there's no way one can live alone there without the other. Best thing for me is not be pushy, just let Philip know I have a passionate interest.

I hate having that ugly thought. Now when I drive by, I'll be like mentally checking their blood pressure. I suspect Philip told them this was my idea hoping that I'd put the screws to them or glad-hand them into thinking I could make them rich beyond their wildest dreams.

By this time Kevin's an hour later than he said he'd be and I'm a little toasted from the wine and tired of waiting, so I cook pasta and Ragu and eat it and decide he can worry about himself. When he gets in, I tell him I couldn't wait, and he says, "Oh, I stopped at Taco Bueno in Plano on the way back," which I accept as an apology for not calling even knowing that Sherrie and Ellen would scream at me for that.

While he's eating two scoops of the butter pecan I bought this very day, I ask, "Kevin, what do you think would keep two people married for over sixty years?"

He gives me this look so I add, "Academic question only."

"Religion," he says.

"Anything else?"

"Habit? Or money, maybe—one has it and the other doesn't."

Kevin's Dad left his Mom after their twenty-eighth anniversary. His Dad wanted to find himself but still hasn't even after five years, and the surprise was that his Mom did and she didn't know she'd be looking.

"Okay, then, happily married."

"Happily married for sixty years? I don't know anybody like that."

"How about the Bundlelays?"

He shrugs and ducks his head toward his bowl. He has really great hair like George Clooney's and he keeps it in a pony-tail with a silver and turquoise clip; he was shooting photos at the Yanni concert for a pr agency—he had on hiking boots and snug jeans and a photographer's vest, and he leaped about nimble as a gymnast to get his shots and he looked so damn cool, you know?

He says, "What makes you think they're happy?"

"Well, they look happy. They act like they're happy together."

"Maybe it's an act. A public face, you know."

I shouldn't let this piss me off, but I realize too late that we're not talking about the Bundlelays. "Why do you need to think they're unhappy?"

"Jesus, Jennifer! I don't need to think anything about them! I don't know them! I'm just going by the odds!"

I get up to water my African violets over my sink so he can't see my face. S & E would approve of that, at least. I say, "My mortgage is due tomorrow," and he says, "My checkbook's out in the car," and I shrug and say, "Whenever," meaning before tomorrow. Kevin pays half the mortgage because he lives here, and we're supposed to split expenses, but I hate to nickel-and-dime somebody. The mortgage actually has fifteen days' grace, so I think I'm really sending him another message.

Befriending Mrs. B makes my conscience grumble—I'm afraid she'll think I'm sucking up to handle the deal, and I'm afraid I'll think that, too. When I call Philip, I tell him I believe that they can be happy only in that house. To me it's a gestalt, the house and their happiness, but that's not anything I can prove—I guess it's what a realtor would think.

I say, "Maybe they need someone to come in every day for a while and clean and cook a little, check on them."

He says, "Oh, I've gone down that road. They said it'd be like having guests all the time." He adds, "I sure would appreciate it if you'd stop by now and then."

He feels free to ask that since I failed him otherwise. I think he's saying he'll keep me at the top of his list if I do.

I say, "Oh sure I will. They're really great! It's wonderful to see a couple stick together like that. They're an inspiration!" I want him to know I'll do it for personal reasons.

I do what he asks and then some. Mr. B has lots of doctors' appointments and Mrs. B isn't much for driving—they have an '85 Buick still showing under a 100K and I don't suppose she drove it much until his sight went so bad everybody was afraid for him to get behind the wheel. I drive them to Presbyterian several times in my Explorer and shuttle them to Walgreen's. I keep telling them I don't mind going alone to pick up their prescriptions, but they say something like, "Oh no! Least we can do is go get them ourselves!" Which makes the trips four times longer. Getting them in and out of the car is worse than strapping in a bunch of toddlers.

Couple times a week I drop by about 4:30 if I have a window between showings and I say like, "Gee, you know, I could sure go for a LuAnn platter down at Luby's—would you join me?" They appreciate this because when you're there before 5:30 everybody in line is like banging along on walkers, canes or crutches, and sure enough the Bs know everyone and more often than not we wind up sharing somebody's table, and believe me by now I am an expert on exactly what happens when you get a hip or a knee replaced. I could assist in a by-pass blindfolded and know like all the loopholes in Medicare and Medicaid.

Once I asked Kevin to come along and he looked at me like I'm out of my mind. I want him to see how they make it through the line and to the table and through the meal and back out to the car with so many little mutual ministrations. There's not a single instant when some part of the one—a finger, a sleeve, an elbow —isn't touching a part of the other. Mostly it's her clinging to him and him using his weight to ease her up and down, in and out. I say clinging but it could be called massaging or stroking. If I have the guts, I'll ask her if they still have sex. Oprah did a show on it. I guess because I think they're such a marvel I want to show them off to the world as a goal for everybody to reach for—hey, a possible standard, that's the point!

They worry about each other like a lot. If they're separated by more than about twenty feet, he calls out, "Evie, you ok?" and she'll say, "Right here, Daddy," and each gives me a run-down on the other's current health when one is out of sight or earshot.

I never hear either cut the other. He tells me her memory is going, but he says it like the loss is his. She says he always expects people to do their best and gets disappointed a lot, but you know she admires him for it.

Mr. B's recuperation is slow, and he has a relapse one night that zips him back to Presbyterian. The son comes in from Las Colinas to stay with his mother, though she insists on sleeping in that hospital chair. I coax her out to dinner at the Black-eyed Pea on Greenville by offering to pick her up at the hospital and to take her back.

She orders beef stew because she can handle it with a spoon but hardly eats a thing.

"He's in good hands, Eveline." I'm leaning over the table so I won't have to shout, and I make my lips easy to read. "Those doctors and nurses they know what they're doing."

"I always have this silly notion that nothing could happen if I'm there," she says. "Or if it does, I sure don't want him to face it all alone."

"Nothing's going to happen. I just know he's going to be okay, really!" Of course, I know no such thing, but it's what you say, isn't it?

She chuckles. "You know he told me that if he goes first, he wants me to find another fellow to look after me."

I smile. "Does he have any candidates?"

She laughs. "Oh, my word, no! Well, there was this friend he knew I was sort of sweet on, but he's been dead for fifteen years."

She picks at her stew while I finish my plate, then out of a silence she says, "I hope he does go first."

I guess my raised brows show my shock. I'm afraid to ask her to explain for fear I'll learn something I don't want to know, and for a tiny instant I see how much I've invested in the idea that happiness with a man is possible.

But I can't help asking, "Really?"

"Yes," she says. "I can't stand to think about how lonely he would be without me."

Her eyes water up. I have this humongous lump in my throat, too. It seems like a good moment to tell her what's in my heart and to see what advice she might give. I tell her how much I admire their mutual devotion and that if I do nothing else in my life but manage to have their kind of marriage, I'll consider myself a great success.

"What do you think has kept you two together all these years?" I ask.

"Oh, hon!" she declares. "I'm sorry but there's nothing I can say that would be of any use to you! Why we're together is just because we're Eveline and Harold and it wouldn't apply for a minute to anybody else. You know how they always ask those old folks on their hundredth birthday what do they owe their longevity to, and they always say the most foolish things! 'Why, I smoked three cigars and drank a pint of whisky every day.' Or they say it's having faith in the Lord or eating turnips!' Truth is they don't have the foggiest."

"You don't think it's because you really love each other?" I might have been whining.

"Of course, we really love each other. But lots of people do that and can't stand to be in the same room for more than five minutes at a time."

I decide to explain about Kevin. I tell her how we met and how he came to live in my house and what I want from a husband—I always wanted a man who will worry about me and my health and welfare, my feelings and my progress through life, who wants to tell me each little thing that happened to him while we're away from one another, who is affectionate and playful and smart and funny. And now and then he can give me a little trinket out of the blue and say it made him think of me and I wouldn't care if it only cost a dollar ninety-eight.

"And is your Kevin like that?"

"Not much."

"Well, does he love you and do you love him?"

I think about her category of people in love who can't stand to be in the same room. I guess Kevin fits it because this is how he acts toward me.

"I guess," I say.

"Aw, hon, I'm sorry!"

She looks so sad for me that I about break down and bawl. "Me too."

"If I do know one thing it's that when it happens you won't be doing any guessing," she says. "You're an awfully good girl. You keep looking, you hear me?"

Mrs. B gets her terrible wish. Mr. B turns for the worst. She's dozing in the chair when he dies in his sleep. Philip tells me, because Mrs. B is so despondent she has to be sedated an inch this side of comatose, and on the day of Mr. B's funeral, just as I'm about to walk down to help her get to the church, her heart defibrillates; the ambulance whizzes past me, and by the time I reach the house they're rushing her out on a gurney with a mask over her face.

Mr. B's funeral goes on without her. We go to hers three days later. I tell you it about wrecks me for a while, I get awfully sentimental thinking about what they stand for in my mind and how maybe they were the Very Last Happily Married Couple.

Kevin changes his schedule so that he's beside me for the second one, even does it without asking. I start thinking about the house again, only not in a greedy way. I mean not greedy for a showcase that will bring me glory as a realtor and home-owner. Maybe greedy for the luck or the feng-shui or the vibes or whatever is in the house that makes me think that living in it could make us happy, me and Kevin. I even worry that redoing the darn thing might jinx us. Or maybe even removing their things would—I have this idea that if I buy the place, I have to keep it as a shrine, turn it into The Museum of Marriage.

And of course, Philip shows up hardly two weeks after Mr. and Mrs. B are buried in Restland north of LBJ. It's a Monday evening after a weekend of two twelve-hour days of showing and gabbing and I've twisted Kevin's arm to help me in the yard. He's running the hedge clippers while I'm on the mower and Philip has to tap me on the shoulder to get my attention.

While the men sit on the porch chairs, I go fix three glasses of iced tea, and when I come back, Kevin is saying, "You know offhand how many square feet are in that attic space?" and Philip says, "Well, it's about the same as the other floors but not all of it's useable because of the roof lines up there," and Kevin says, "Is there flooring or just the bare rafters?" and Philip says, "Oh, it's fully floored. Old pine, great stuff, about yay wide" and holds his index fingers apart in the air.

I don't know who brought up the subject. But when I serve their tea, Philip says, "Jennifer, I don't want to seem premature, but soon as the will gets probated, we can start the ball rolling about the house."

I get this terrible knot in my stomach. "Have you thought about keeping it in the family, Philip? You and your wife could make it a beautiful showcase, you know. Or maybe one of your children would like to keep it."

He grew up there and surely has a soft spot for it. Or I think he should, at least.

"Well, sentiment aside, it's the difference between getting a few hundred grand and spending one."

Kevin says, "Do remember if there are outlets up there or not?"

Philip says, "Well, there's an overhead fixture, you know a pull chain with just a bulb, so the service does go up there."

Kevin says, "You suppose it'd be much trouble to run a water line up from the second-floor bathroom?"

"Probably not," says Philip. "Drain, too. You thinking about a dark room?"

"And a studio."

We sit watching neighbors come and go in their yards, to their cars. One thing about living in houses that don't have attached garages—people have to show themselves. Kevin's foot is jittering against the decking; he's excited. Philip keeps looking up the sidewalk as if expecting somebody—Mr. and Mrs. B?—but it turns out it will be his wife walking up to tell him she's ready to head home to Las Colinas.

He asks about a contract, and I say, "Gee, Philip, I'm really sorry, but this is an incredibly busy time for me. How about I talk to another of our agents about handling the house? I know some-body who will really do a great job for you," and I give him a verbal resume of our agency's top producer.

He shrugs, agrees out of politeness to receive the call, says good evening and strolls down the walk to meet his wife.

"Wow!" says Kevin. "I thought you'd shoot your granny for a chance to sell that house! I thought you wanted to buy it. Is it like a conflict of interest or something?"

"Yes, it's like a conflict of interest."

"So will you make an offer on it?"

"I don't think so."

He is totally baffled. I'm a little surprised myself. "Really?"

"Really. Why don't you buy it and redo it!"

"Me?"

"Why not? You make enough money."

"Well, I just never thought about being a home-owner."

"I see," I say. "But you think of yourself as someone who lives in a home, am I right?"

We're silent for a bit. He's like bewildered by this turn. Finally, he says, "I just figured you'd buy it and fix it up. You were talking about it. And I'd help. Just like you said, we'd have more space."

"Tell you what," I say, "You buy it and fix it up, then you ask me to come live with you there."

"Would you? You would, wouldn't you?"

"I honestly don't know. Maybe so, maybe no. It's a risk you'd have to take."

"Aw, I know you would," he says. "That house? You'd do it."

"You never know," I say.

Familiar Strangers

I woke up here a while ago. I look into the cupboards for things I expect to find, so I'm guessing I live here. I've got other evidence, too: the table I'm writing on now is a square plate of steel propped atop four tree stumps buried in white sand, and I know without looking that the underside is coated with layers of peeling paint. Maybe in the past I made a decision about which side to place up.

I can't figure out why I know some things and don't know others. Looking out the door to this hut, I see birds pecking at dead fish washed up on the beach. "Sandpipers," I think, but I don't know for sure. I know without opening the door to the chest hanging on the wall that it contains fish line, three rusty hooks, a broken transistor radio, and a bottle of iodine with the label obscured by spillage ... But I don't know who I am and how I came to be here.

I spent most of the morning learning what I seem to have known already. For instance, when I got tired of standing while I was thinking, I eased down on an old car seat positioned against the seaside wall of the hut, and I was careful not to sit on the sunken end because I knew the springs were broken there and a loose end would stick through the stuffing if I put my weight on it. I learned that I knew that when I'm hungry I can dig canned goods out of the cardboard box that's covered with a piece of torn canvas ... After I had gone through most of the boxes and looked through drawers and cupboards, I felt a little better. I can say I sort of belong here. At least I know enough now to stay alive, but not what for.

Around twilight last night I was starting to feel comfortable. I tidied up the room, dug out some candles from the toolbox under the table, and was wondering where I kept the matches. Suddenly a man was standing in the door! I jumped behind the table and grabbed my ax for protection. Who are you and what do you want? I yelled at him. It was too dark to see his face clearly, but he had a familiar presence—I might have known him a long time ago, but hadn't thought of him in years. He was holding something in his hands. Here, he said. Have a naked breast. He dropped it to the sand and disappeared. The thing formed a dim hump on the sand by the door. I found the matches where I imagined I had left them, in an old tobacco can, lit a candle, and inspected the hump. It was a butt of uncooked ham, its flat, sawed surface bleeding. It was repulsive. I kicked it out the door.

All that really upset me. Unless I just imagined the man, other people live around here, and I'm not sure I'd like them if I got to know them. Just when I had started to feel... positioned, he showed up and disturbed the flow between information received and information analyzed. His visit put me too heavy on the input side. Kept me awake most of the night worrying.

I did sleep for a while, though. I had dreams. I remember an apartment in a large city. Luxurious, tasteful, civilized. Through a window you can watch lights work their way up through a mist. In the living room, the decor is modern. Having a drink. A woman is beside me on the white sofa; she seems familiar enough that I don't look at her when she speaks, although I know she's attractive. Our host and his wife sit across from us in chairs with chartreuse and tangerine leather covers. They seem at ease. They're laughing at something I've said; I'm laughing, too, then I add, "You have to admit that's pretty good for a man who makes a living lying about ice cream," and they laugh again, but differently. It's as if I've said something they agree with but wouldn't have said themselves because it wouldn't have been polite.

Other hazy images are disconnected. It's funny how I'm in the habit of saying to myself, "I had a lot of dreams last night," thinking of separate images as individual dreams. But wouldn't it make just as much sense to say that from the time I fall asleep to the time I wake up that any dreaming I do is all of a piece? Or that the dreams I have on separate nights are really one dream unified by me the dreamer? After all, I don't think of my waking life in daily segments, I don't say "I lived on Monday and again on Tuesday." I can feel a continuity there, so why not in my dream life? Just as I can say, "I've been having a conscious life ever since I was born," I can say I've been having a dream for just as long, and not mean a recurring dream. A continuous dream.

I'm getting scared in this place. I hope that's because I don't understand it, know my own place in it, how I got here, how long I've been here, how long it'll last. I keep shivering and sweating when I think about it. This place is like some territory out in the ocean where nothing happens and you're always lost—the Horse Latitudes—and you can't sail out of it because there's no wind. Only this is dry land.

Maybe if I can find some answers I'll feel better. This morning I remembered Robinson Crusoe's joy when he found a footprint in the sand. I'm not sure there's a comparison between us. I know this island (how do I know it's an island?) is inhabited. I mean I think it is. Right after I woke up this morning I went to the door of the hut and the ham was gone, but I don't know if the man returned for it, or an animal carried it off, or whether I just dreamed it up. I feel better thinking maybe it hadn't happened.

I didn't realize how afraid I was until it occurred to me that since waking up here I hadn't left the hut. I'd been feeling like a prisoner with nonexistent jailers. That ambivalence—the security of a cell, that tiny piece of territory assigned to me.

The sea seemed safe, so in the middle of the afternoon I left the hut and walked out to the beach. I'm not sure of the season, but it feels like summer—a sky the color of acetylene flame, flat clouds swimming like puffy cartoon bubbles in a hot blue milk; a thick, wet onshore breeze, and a sun so strong it numbs my mind and blinds me. On the beach I found a beer can. So there are people around! That didn't mean the man with the ham had been real, necessarily. But it did get me to thinking that maybe somebody around here could answer my questions. On the other hand, if they're like the man who came to my hut, I'm not sure I want to ask. Maybe I was a member of their community and they put me on this "reservation." Maybe I broke a law. Maybe they're watching me from the fringes of the dunes behind the hut. Many possibilities. Maybe I'm a madman experiencing periodic sanity; maybe when I wake up tomorrow, I won't remember today, just as when I woke up the day before yesterday, I didn't remember my previous life here but did see evidence that I'd lived it. If that's the case, then maybe my best shot would be to contact them for help. I can see them shouting, "The fever has broken!" when I stumble into their camp.

On the other hand, maybe they'd shoot me.

I went back to the hut where I sat facing the door with the ax in my lap. All afternoon and into the night.

This morning I worked up the nerve to go swimming. I stood in knee-high surf, looking out to sea, then I turned around to keep my eyes on the hut and started wading backward into deeper water until I couldn't touch bottom. The water felt cool and relaxing, so I began swimming on my back with my head out to sea so I could watch the hut. When I got tired, I started treading water, watching the swells in front of me roll into the beach. All at once an undertow grabbed my hips. Something like kelp twined around my legs, a cold snout poked at my back, a jellyfish brushed my shoulder. I started to fight, got a raw mouthful of salty water, rolled over on my stomach, and thrashed my way toward shore, flailing at the water, panicky, and when I reached the point where I could stand, I struggled through

43

the surf and fell onto the beach to catch my breath, digging my fingers into the wet sand.

A little later—maybe I dozed—I saw two girls wading in the surf about a hundred yards to my right. They moved up onto the beach and stooped to collect something. Beachcombing, maybe. They looked harmless enough, so I got up and walked toward them. As I got closer I could hear them chattering, but the breeze carried their words away before I could tell what language they were speaking. They were wearing bikinis. One half-turned toward me and I saw a slim profile with small breasts. When she saw me, she spoke to the other, and they both turned their heads and skipped away. I yelled for them to wait, but they broke into a run, so I came to a stop. They might be lures. An ambush might be waiting around the next bend.

The dream goes on. I've started searching it for clues to my name, age, place of birth, marital status, social security number, occupation—anything definite. The stuff here in the hut could belong to anybody—I've searched everything for identifying marks. I had thought that maybe among all the containers in the hut one might have held something to help me. I discovered a small metal box in the bottom of one of the three footlockers. Its lid had a built-in lock. Because it looked like something used for keeping documents safe, I tried for several minutes to pry it open with a knife, getting all excited about it. I had to take a screwdriver and a ballpeen hammer and whack away at the lock to get the box open. It held only a sliver of a broken mirror, like something left behind when the other contents were removed. It's possible, I guess, that the sliver was placed there for safekeeping—I mean, I can't be too careful about what I presume—but it doesn't seem likely. My point is that I've exhausted all possibility of these tangibles giving me any idea about myself.

In the dream, I'd guess my host to be about forty. If I think hard maybe I can recall somebody calling me by name. Does the hostess say, "Can I get you another drink, _____?" I seem to be getting my own drinks. Quite a few of them. It's all hazy. I've decided, though, that the woman beside me on the couch is my wife. Call it an educated guess: (1) I'm not nervous or self-conscious with her; I don't get tense when our thighs touch; (2) our host and hostess seem to know us both equally well, or hardly at all; (3) as I said before, I don't feel I have to turn toward her when she talks, I don't have to convince her of my attention or disguise my inattention; (4) at one point she whispers something indistinguishable in my ear. I wonder if we have children. Of course, we could be old friends, brother and sister.

I'm confused about the condition of the room. Sometimes I see empty trays whose bottoms are littered with peanut skins and empty cocktail glasses standing on damp napkins, ashtrays stuffed with butts. Then the room is clean, everything put away. Maybe the woman and I were the first to arrive and the last to leave. Maybe a maid straightened up after the party. A maid suggests money. Our friend, the host, must have money. Maybe I do too, being his friend. Now that I think of it, my clothes are expensive, they fit well, even though I'm uncomfortable in them—it's as though I'm accustomed to feeling uncomfortable in them. They seem to restrain me. From what, I don't know.

I'm pleased with the dream. I've got it worked out so that I can use a kind of valve in my head to let a bit of the dream flow into consciousness where I can take a look at it, and when the content threatens to overwhelm my ability to sort out the information, the valve shuts off, like the float in a toilet tank. At first, a couple days ago I tried to recall as much of the dream in one sitting as I could, but that just got me racing from one thought to the next. Taking it a little at a time is teaching me patience; it's as if the details of my life are a murder mystery I'm reading and I'm not going to flip over to the end to find out who done it before I get there.

I made contact with the people on the island! I have to back up a bit to describe it, though. Along toward noon I had gotten bored with my dream. That I could be bored in the middle of this mystery about myself really scared me. What if I give up the search? What if this business about the "valve" is only a clever way of deceiving myself so that I can't get at the truth? What if I'm becoming so adjusted here that I don't care how I got here or who I am? I don't know how long I'll be "awake"; I could lapse into another spell of "amnesia" at any time and have to start all over again. Maybe before that morning four days ago I knew all about who I was and what I am; or maybe I only knew as much as I know now, and I've been starting over endlessly for a number of years. And getting only so far before "forgetting." I thought at first that this journal would help, so that if things get foggy again, at least when I "woke" I'd have something solid to hang onto. But it's also possible—I was thinking —that I've made records in the past that "they" take away from me when I "sleep."

It's no mystery why I left the hut.

As soon as I stepped out the door, I saw an old man in faded bathing trunks hunkering on the beach. He was looking out to sea. One arm was wrapped around his knees, the other positioned so that his hand held a conch shell to his ear. He rocked back and forth, from side to side, more like a steady swaying, really. I wanted to yell at him, but I decided to be careful. I didn't want to get caught in an ambush, even though I didn't have any evidence that anybody was out to do me harm, any evidence except my fear, that is, which I think is reason enough. So I waited a few minutes at the door to the hut, watching him sway. Then I walked toward him, slowly, ready to run, keeping an eye on the line of vegetation behind the dunes. When I got to within a few yards, I called out as politely as I could. "Hey there!" I said. He didn't seem to hear me.

I walked up to him from the rear and stood for a second clearing my throat. I thought the conch kept him from hearing me, so I reached down and touched him lightly on the shoulder. This wasn't something I ordinarily would've done, but I thought the situation called for it. He didn't even look around; he simply passed his arm across his shoulder and grasped my hand in his. His skin was dry and cool, like silk. I was embarrassed—he thought I was someone else. I tried tugging my hand away, but he held on tightly, not looking at me. "Excuse me!" I shouted.

He turned his face toward mine. He'd been crying. I guessed that I'd stumbled onto another man's private grief, so I began apologizing, but the more I explained, the more I saw he didn't understand me. He smiled back at me like a child, his withered skin sliding and folding along his face.

Where do you come from? I asked slowly. I pointed in three different directions away from the sea. There? There? Or there?

Smiling, nodding, he held out the conch for me to take as though it were a telephone and somebody on the other end would give me the answer.

What's your name? No response. Only that moronic smile. I'd have to get him to leave, then follow. I straightened up and made shooing motions with my hands. Go on! I said. Go home now!

He looked bewildered, then frightened. I really didn't want to scare him, but I had to get him to go. I grimaced and cocked my fist. He scrambled up and began trotting off down the beach, looking over his shoulder. When I followed, he broke into a trot out of fear, so I slowed down to give him a little lead.

He disappeared into the undergrowth behind the dunes, and I trailed him, trying to keep out of sight so he wouldn't panic. I followed his tracks for about a mile until I saw him go over a dune whose seaward side led down to the beach. As I got near the top of the dune I could hear voices, so I dropped down onto the sand. Had I been trapped?

I crept up the side of the dune and peeked over its crest.

People! Maybe thirty or forty gathered on the beach. On spread blankets I saw hunks of beef and pork and loaves of bread and bottles of wine and cheeses and cakes as big as basketballs! Nobody seemed interested in me. A volleyball game was in progress; the two girls I had seen alone on the beach were supervising the construction of an immense sand castle being built by a half-dozen younger children; the old man I had tracked to this spot now hunkered at the edge of the sea with the conch to his ear—I watched a young woman get up from an ice chest, walk down to the old man, and drape a towel across his shoulders. Three other children were burying a man up to his neck in the sand while a woman held a newspaper over his head to shade him and offered him sips from a bottle of wine. At the edge of the crowd, a young couple lay face to face on a blanket, noses touching. The volleyball players—all young men—postured and flexed for an audience of young women who lay preening and baking on the sand where the surf touched once in ten waves or so, running in rivulets between their legs, tickling them and making them giggle.

A man in undershirt and slacks with the legs rolled up to his knees lay on his back in the sand. He bounced a little girl in a red bathing suit on his belly. When he lifted her, she laughed and her gold hair flashed in the light. A woman lay beside them, propped on an elbow, her feet bare, her dress tangled about her thighs. She was talking to the man. They laughed, then the child laughed, and then they laughed at the child's laughing at their laughter. The woman's hair was light brown and it swirled around her shoulders as she stroked the man's hair back from his forehead. Her right foot idly pushed the sand at her feet into a mound, and her toes scooped out a hollow, steadily, absently, like a cow chewing its cud.

I jumped up and ran back to the hut as fast as I could.

I wish I knew what it was about the man and his wife and the child that shook me up so much. The reel in my memory of that scene keeps hanging on frozen frames—the man with his trousers rolled to his knees, the woman's hair moving over her shoulders, the child's hair flashing in the light. Over and over. I can't make any sense out of my obsession with them. Where do they live? What are their names? Where does he work? Why aren't they wearing bathing suits? How long have they been married? No matter how much I try to study them, their private lives are as remote to me as the lives of a trio of musicians playing a concert. I see them laugh, their hair, their limbs, the way their limbs cross over and touch each other. I play the man, feel the wet, sandy bottom of the girl's bathing suit across my stomach, her weight on my ribs, her tiny hands grabbing my fingers for support, the woman's palm caressing my forehead, her hair blowing gently against my cheek, the soft curve of her breast against my arm—there, now, I am the man: what's my name? Nothing. Then I'm the woman—I feel the man's brow under my hand, the sand between my toes, the hem of my skirt shifting against my thigh in the breeze, my breast against his arm, my own laughter in my chest. But no name.

Watching them seems like a dream now. I remember a spasm in my body urging me across the dune and into the party. It scared me. I think that's why I ran. When I got back to the hut, I found sand crusted on my cheeks, proving to me that I had cried, but I don't know for sure. Or why. It could have been sweat.

Why would I have cried? These things worry me; I'm afraid I won't get out of here before I fall asleep again. The distance between us is agonizing—why are they there and I here? What rules govern us? I feel very... bitter now, my eyes threaten to betray me again. A small boy, lost someplace—where was it? A clue? No, all I remember is feeling abandoned, as though I had gotten lost at a carnival or a supermarket, and I feel that sudden rush of hopelessness, loss, and separation.

I've decided that I might be lonely. Deciding that gave me an insight. Looking back through the journal, I found this sentence: "I didn't realize how afraid I was until it occurred to me that I hadn't left the hut since waking up." Although I don't know my name or social security number or how I got here or what my life means or when I'll die, I do know this, now - I seem to have a hard time recognizing it when I feel things. I seem to figure out I felt a certain way based on how I acted, then sort of deduce how I was feeling. I seem to be blind to it while it's happening. That's why I "decide" that "maybe I might" be lonely. I guess I am.

I am.

The cocktail party is in progress. Maybe fifty people are milling around my friends' apartment. Hands. Seem to be thousands of hands everywhere. As I go from person to person I see long, short, stubby, wide, narrow, weak, pale, dark. Many more thousands of fingers with rings of assorted colors weights widths. Hands and fingers closed around cylinders, hands to display lighted cigarettes, gesturing. Over in a corner a woman brushes red fingertips across a man's forearm as she talks; a man on the sofa massages the back of his neck, his hand broad, freckled with reddish blond hair sprouting on the knuckles; a woman opposite him lets her fingers fly to her cheek, to her breasts, then back to her cheek, as though pointing out her features; near the kitchen doorway a man talking to a woman crosses his arms and presses his hand into his armpits, hiding them, restraining them, while the woman's left hand grips a small glass and her right hand is knotted at her waistline and held in place by the pressure of her left elbow. A man near me pinches his nose, another tugs at his moustache, and another surreptitiously rearranges his balls. The women's hands grow more exotic, more surreal, like birds captured at the ends of wrists—hummingbirds with plumage marked by a small gold band rushing to tips of plum; a common sparrow, a chicken, a pheasant. Nails curved, hooked, broken, split, painted, rounded, torn, pointed. And the hands grow until they are as large as trashcan lids and everyone finds them cumbersome as they use them for shields.

Time slows down, motion becomes sluggish as though this is all happening underwater, and the strange elephantiasis which struck first in their hands now moves on to their mouths. Faces become merely the frame for exhibiting mouths, tongues, lips and teeth; their voices rise as their mouths balloon into swollen shapes, wet and sucking, then recede...

Later I'm on the balcony overlooking the city and a woman is with me, very drunk, muttering to herself. Not exactly with me. Adjacent to me. I don't exactly recognize her, but she might be "Janet," the wife of a guy I know slightly, but I'm wondering if she isn't another woman who bears a similarity to "Janet." I'm drunk, too, but I think I'm more sober than she. I speak to her. I call her "Janet." She turns to me and... simpers, but she's not responding to the name, just to the voice. I'm not even sure if the wife of the acquaintance is named "Janet," and I'm less sure whether this is the "Janet" I'm thinking of. She's very attractive. Her eyes are glazed; she runs the tip of her tongue across her upper lip. George! she whispers, as if to say at last we meet again! The name seems remote to me. I'm pretty sure that she thinks at heart I'm really not "George." I kiss her mouth, my left hand strokes her breast, she presses against my leg. I'm almost overwhelmed by wanting her—she's a river of warm oil I want to sink and drown in. In the middle of the kiss, she almost loses her balance and throws her foot out suddenly to right herself. That awkward motion brings me back to the fact that I'm kissing a stranger who I'm pretending to myself is the wife of a man I slightly know, while she's kissing someone she's pretending is "George"; so there is who I am and who I am pretending to be ("George") and who she is pretending me to be ("Maybe George")—all three of me kissing who she is and who she is pretending to be ("Janet") and who I'm pretending her to be ("Maybe Janet"). The embrace grows so complicated, so sad, really, that I break off and hold her in my arms, pitying us both, whoever we are, and she says, in my ear, not surprised or shocked, but as though she is just voicing a motion of her mind: you're not George!

I'm not George!

A clue. While I stand dumbfounded, she slips out of my embrace and eases away, not in anger, more like drifting while I stand thinking over and over, I am not George! It's almost something I could wear on a name tag.

When I come off the balcony I'm a different man. A changed man. I stand at the threshold looking on the party, sneering at the guests: I am not George! It's as though a god has stooped to touch my brow. The empty chatter. People are putting things into their mouths, stuffing, drooling—cigarettes, glasses, sandwiches, toothpicks, pipes, crackers, olives, cigars, their own fingers, other people's fingers, pickles, tiny fish, pieces of pig, chunks of unborn chicken—what a monstrous and pitiful hunger!

Then the room is empty except for the woman who was beside me on the couch much earlier (my "wife"), and the host and hostess are putting on their coats and leaving (?), and the host drunkenly leans toward me, shakes my hand, and says, great party, thanks for... Then I'm in a dark room, a bedroom, and I'm in the bed longing for a woman's touch, feeling sad for all those people at the party, the woman on the balcony; in my not-Georgeness I feel guilty at my own contempt, so I bathe them in my compassion as recompense. Then all at once I feel the same bitterness I felt when I watched the people on the beach. I feel the bed dip slightly as the woman who had been beside me on the couch sits on it, smelling of soap and sweat and half-washed perfume, and, remembering the woman on the balcony, I want to sink into that river again, but I feel my hands shrinking, my lips shrinking, and the more I try to reach out for her the more my hands grow smaller by the second, my lips draw up, and my voice contracts into a tiny peep deep inside my gut even though I'm trying to cry out as loud as I can. The bed quivers and the woman's shoulders jerk; I can tell she is crying, and I know it's for me, but not for the tragic hero that I feel is me, but for the child she thinks is me—she's weeping in pity, and she says, "I'm sorry, I'm sorry," apologizing not for something done, but something she cannot do; and I know she means you must touch to be touched.

Caustic

The blind man got home a little after 6 p.m. after an hour's trip requiring a bus transfer, exited the elevator on the sixth floor, and stepped off his habitual 16 paces to the left along the hall. His graphite folding cane oscillated across his path like the sensitive antenna of an insect but did not alert his hand to anything amiss.

He unlocked the door, let himself in, closed and relocked it. He broke his cane down into its three attached pieces, but when he reached to set the bundle on the straight chair right there against the wall, he knocked his knuckles on a large metal structure and the cane clattered to the floor. His heart thumped, tripped a beat. He stood paralyzed in shock for a moment. Where was he? It was as if he'd fallen asleep and had awakened in a strange room and couldn't place it. His mind bumped against the fact of the door, his door, that he'd unlocked so easily.

He took several deep, slow breaths. The apartment air carried the faint hint of the peel from the banana he'd eaten for breakfast and dropped into the trash under the sink, though, unbeknownst to him, that can with its wet refuse now festered under his living room window. A kind of interior barometric pressure informed him that the walls stood at their usual distance from the door.

What was this object he'd rapped his knuckles on? He turned, slowly, to his left, raised his palm as if to stop the thing or shield his face, then advanced it inch by inch. It met that surface again. He moved to find the upper limit, then left and right to determine size and shape. Shortly, he knew this thing to be his refrigerator. Not running. Not plugged in, he guessed.

Why was it beside the door? Who had moved it and why?

The blind man was accustomed to encountering the unknown, as it was a prominent feature of his daily life. It lay perpetually just outside the reach of the definite, that territory circumscribed by his mind's eye recreating what experience had previously fashioned. Just across the nearby perimeter, if he should happen there by accident, say, lurked disorientation and danger. You might hear a bus or truck roaring toward you but not know which way to leap. Someone says can I help you when maybe they mean to do you harm. You are safe only by treading the very narrow path scribed in your imagination by practice.

He had less experience with an unexpected unknown such as the one he was presently swimming in while standing in his foyer with his coat still on. This business about the refrigerator and the straight chair baffled him, but he didn't know how deeply this oddity extended into the apartment. He knelt and felt about for the cane, retrieved it, inserted the sections in place, stood. He then moved one step forward, but the cane struck something solid in a location where only benign air normally welcomed him. He pressed the cane's tip against it and followed the shaft down to feel the thing— the hassock to the easy chair in his living room. He might've tripped over it, the way it was square in his usual path. This mad jumble could be wall to wall.

He patted the breast of his blazer to make sure his phone was still pocketed there, as if this strange scrambling of the ordinary might've mysteriously spread to his very person. And it was, thank God, right there. He crabbed it free and gripped it in his fist. His sister was but a touch away on his speed dial. But after a moment of breathing quietly and listening to the water drip in the bathroom sink, the caged parrots squawk in the apartment next door, and the trucks rumble past on the street below, he was fairly certain his place was empty but for him and his problem.

Suddenly he shuddered. "Millie!?" he called. "Where are you?" He pictured people moving the furniture and Millie scampering between their legs and out the door. Mostly likely, though, any intruders had terrified her into hiding inside her own familiar place. "Millie!!" He stood still as he could and listened. He had to resist thrashing headlong through the jungle of misplaced furniture.

He edged forward slowly, using his cane and his free hand, encountering objects and recognizing them, visualizing their places so that a revised choreography of this new life in a bewildering maze of misplaced things might be crudely fashioned for temporary use. Step by step he explored the living room. His bed, the covers utterly disheveled and the pillows missing, now stood in the center of the carpet. Books, CDs, and articles of clothing strewn on the floor confounded his steps into a slow, cautious shuffle; he pigeon-toed forward, his soles canted to plow the path ahead.

He barked his shin on his trunk when he turned abruptly toward his bedroom and bath, bumped a knee on a clothes hamper unexpectedly lurking in the hall, then, more carefully, he took to tapping his cane on the walls as well as he inched along like a miner whose lamp had gone out.

"Millie!" he called again, stopped, listened, heard nothing, groped his way to the doorframe of his bedroom, edged into the room, then his cane immediately poked the end of his sofa. He laid a hand along the back of it and kept shuffling deeper into the mystery; he jostled the kitty litter tray balanced on the sofa's back, upending it and spilling its contents onto the seat cushions and his shoes.

He called continually, stopping to listen, his breath shallow. After another half hour of tagging familiar items found in wholly unexpected places, he reached the bathroom doorway. "Millie!" Then he heard a single plaintive meow echo in the room, and he dropped to his knees and crawled about, discovering as he did that his breakfast table now straddled the hips of the old claw-footed tub.

At last, he located her behind the tub, in a corner, so terrified that when he plucked her up from where she cowered, she squirmed and bit the heel of his hand. But he persisted and held her firmly, stroked her to a state of calm, murmuring, "It's all right, kitty." However, when he held her a certain way, she struggled and jerked about, as if she'd been bruised or injured during the uproar. Perhaps she'd been roughly handled or something had fallen on her.

He sat awhile on the closed toilet lid holding the cat and letting his breath settle. His mantle clock chimed seven, though from somewhere other than the living room shelf it normally spoke from. He realized he hadn't eaten since lunch. Carrying the cat, he made his way to his bedroom closet, opened the door, knew immediately that nothing had been touched, reached down to the floor and retrieved a pet carrier and slipped the cat into it. He thought she would welcome the confinement of known space.

He retraced his steps back into the living room, where he groped behind the refrigerator for the cord, then felt the wall for the outlet, and plugged in the box. He probed the interior and was relieved that nothing had apparently been removed or added, though things had been jostled. He stood beside the open door and drank from a carton of milk, pulled an apple from the hydrator. He moved to his sink and opened a cabinet door, set his fingers fluting lightly over the jars and boxes on the shelves, noting that this odd plague of displacement had not seeped through the cabinet doors. He took out his peanut butter and stood eating from the jar with his fingers, alternating the scoops of oily butter with bites from the apple.

By now he'd removed his overcoat and blazer. When he no longer felt shaky from hunger, he made his way back into his bedroom with his hands out before him as if parting brambles and sat on the couch, feeling the granules of litter crunch under his soles.

He called his sister and, making a special effort to sound calm, told her what he'd encountered but didn't mention the condition of his pet.

"Oh, my word!" It sounded as if she might be saying What next?? "You're all right, aren't you?"

"Yes. But would you do me a favor?" He paused, then went quickly on, "Would you mind calling someone to come tomorrow morning and help me? I'd appreciate it. I can do the small stuff, that's no problem, but I need a hand with the heavier pieces."

"Of course. If you'd like, maybe you could come over here for the night. Frank's not home yet from a meeting, but I can call and ask him to drop by on his way. I'll have to put clean sheets on the guest bed and clean that bathroom, though, because Mildred just left and I haven't had time to fool with it."

"Oh, no! Thanks, anyway. I do have a bed. My bed. It's just not in its usual place. I found it in the living room." That sounded comical to his ears, but he didn't laugh. He didn't want to tell her that he hated to leave Millie here alone again. His sister was allergic to cats, among other things.

"Whatever suits you." Then she said, as if just now thinking of it, "Who would do such a thing? Do you think it's some kind of mistake? Or maybe a prank?"

"I suppose so."

"Well, it's certainly inconsiderate! Making all that extra work for people. Do you have any idea at all who might do this?"

"No, none at all."

"Ah," said the boy. "Pet it prince. Jay cumpriss, pew aye pew, antsy, tah pet it vye melon, melon coah." The boy stopped.

"Meh-lahn-KOAL-eek," said the teacher. He waited, seemingly for the boy to repeat it, but the boy only sat helplessly.

"Do you know what this passage is saying?"

The boy looked toward the classroom door, where, from behind a large window in the top, faces watched him.

"Something about the sunset."

"Yes. And what about it?"

"He likes them," said the boy, grudgingly. His face burned and he turned toward the exterior windows to avoid having to look again at the door.

"Yes. Can you find the line that says this?"

The boy peered at the text open on the desk. Finding the line was no great feat, but the teacher meant for him to say it aloud. That made him cringe, though those at the door likely couldn't hear him. "Jim ben lays cow-shers day sole aisle," he murmured.

"That's it. The pronunciation needs work, but it's good to see you know the vocabulary."

The boy smiled to himself: he was using a text whose previous owner had painstakingly scribed the English translation between the lines of French.

In the window, a hand jabbed a finger at him, a little menacingly.

"Listen, Mister Baldwin, could I go to the restroom real quick? It's like distracting me from concentrating."

"Yes. If you must." The teacher slid his hand along his desk, dropped it down to a handle, pulled a drawer open, sent his fingers skittering across objects there. This was always interesting to watch. It was like the finger action of the crew of Voyager or Battlestar Galactica on their ship's computers, barely touching, speed freak secretaries typing in fast-forward.

Though the school day was over so the pass wasn't necessary, the teacher handed him a stick painted with red and white stripes. The boy rose as if to move toward the door, but he stopped momentarily at the corner of the teacher's desk to furtively drape his hand over the teacher's key ring lying there in the open. As he drew it carefully and silently into his fist, he declared, loudly, "I'll be right back, Mr. Baldwin, I promise. It's just number one, you know."

"I'll be here."

The boy left the room. The hall outside the room was quiet. Three other boys hovered by the door. Wordlessly, the boy handed over the key ring and the others dashed away, stifling giggles as they ran.

The boy watched them disappear. His legs were quivering and he felt a little dizzy. Rank nerve sweat steamed like acid in his pits and stunk like a dog house, he thought. He blew out a breath.

He headed for the restroom—not the one near the classroom but on the next floor up and down a hall, making a trek out of what would've been only a few steps. It would take them about ten to fifteen minutes to get to Ace hardware and back, if the store wasn't busy. The restroom was empty. It was spooky. He took a piss just to use up time. He could imagine someone creeping up to his back while he stood at the urinal. A killer could be in the stall behind him standing on the toilet and waiting for him to unzip. Or maybe Mr. Rockwall would tiptoe in to score a tasty morsel. Was old Baldwin a fag, too? What kind of sex did a blind man have, anyway?

He washed his hands, turned to the towel dispenser only to find it empty, cursed, wiped his hands on his khaki uniform pants. He put in face time with his face. He wished he had thick dark hair because then he'd have a beard already. Pimples all over his fore-head like ants had crawled up there and gotten stuck.

He trudged toward the classroom, gawking at bulletin boards, dawdling, passing a few straggler kids like himself and some teachers, hello-ing them all innocently. When he got back, the others hadn't returned, and he panicked. But he braced himself, went inside. Baldwin was wearing the ear-buds to his iPod and nodding to a beat—what kind of tunes did a blind man like, anyway?

The teacher heard him come in and popped them out.

"Sorry it took so long. They had our restroom like closed for repairs or something and I had to go upstairs." He set the stick down on the desk loud enough that the teacher found it readily and returned it to the drawer.

"It's all right. I believe we have some time left."

"Yes," said the boy. "But I don't mind staying late." He grit his teeth and stared toward the door, conjuring faces in the window.

"Listen, Mr. Baldwin, would you mind doing me a favor?"

"What's that, Christopher?"

"Well, you know you said my pronunciation really sucks. And I was thinking maybe you wouldn't mind reading—I mean reciting—stuff from the book so I can hear it. I would really appreciate it." Baldwin seemed to have whole passages memorized, so the boy could sit listening as long as it took.

"Yes, I could do that. Why don't you follow along as I recite from the first chapter so that you can associate the word with the sound. I rely on you to let me know if I go off course."

"Okay." The boy rifled the pages as if he were turning to chapter one. "I'm ready, sir, whenever you are."

The teacher tilted his face toward the ceiling as if sunshine up there rained down on him. Though he wore dark glasses like any other blind person, when he made this pose, the boy saw under the rims that his eyelids were closed. That struck him as peculiar. If you're blind, why bother?

The teacher began reciting the French text. He had no difficulty remembering, and it quickly became boring to listen without any comprehension. The boy half-wished he'd opened the text to follow along to keep from being driven into a coma, but it was too late, and even if he managed to open it quietly, he probably couldn't find the place. Instead, as the teacher droned on, minute after minute, the boy amused himself by mugging at him, contorting his body, making dance-like gestures in the air with his arms, bobbing his head as if to music, wagging his tongue. He raised his middle finger to each and every wall. He rolled his eyes. He wished the others were there to watch.

There was knock on the door. The teacher stopped reciting and rotated his face toward the sound. One of the other boys came in, grinning, dangling Baldwin's key ring.

"Scuse me, Mr. Baldwin. It's Toby Nedermeyer. I need to get something from Chris, if that's okay."

"All right. I believe our time is up, anyway. I'm sure Christopher has heard enough."

"No, that's cool," the boy made himself say.

The other boy gingerly set the teacher's keys on the desk.

The blind man's brother-in-law sat on the board of Trinity Christian Academy, and the blind man's sister had urged him to get her brother hired so he wouldn't have to borrow money in an emergency. The faith-based facility in an "urban environment" advertised itself as an institution that "fosters family values and recognizes that all students and adolescents in particular best make academic progress where they receive the special attention required to nurture their unique individual talents and needs."

The blind man had taught part-time for three years to supplement his disability payments from Social Security. He tutored individuals and small groups in French, Spanish, Italian and, very occasionally, Latin, and though he held no classes, he was generally at the school for half the day and sometimes served as a substitute teacher. He was given conference periods and a free hour. For the first year, he was content to think that, despite the awkwardness in having constant daily contact with so many sighted young people, he was making a contribution, however small. He didn't have the ease with his students that many faculty seemed to have—joking with them, arguing or teasing and cajoling, using their nicknames, identifying who they "hung with," what music they listened to and knowing the multitude of stars on the TV programs they favored. Around the students, he felt awkward and very self-conscious, stiffly frozen behind a protective screen of protocol and professional distance. He was, he knew, absolutely no fun—they'd never say about him, as they did one of his colleagues, that he was "one cool dude," but he'd believed that being respectful and business-like established an appropriate setting for learning.

One day when he was talking to the payroll clerk about his W-4 deductions, she said, casually, "Too bad the check you get isn't as big as the check we get." He asked what she meant. She told him that because of his special circumstance his position was funded by grants from various governmental agencies. So, the school got $35 an hour for him, even for conference and free periods, and then parents of his students kicked in another $15 an hour for individual lessons. As if realizing she'd been indiscreet, she backpedaled. "Of course, you know, with the handicapped it's different." She spoke as if in sympathy with his blindness or to suggest that the presence of the handicapped suspended normal rules of fairness. She might've been trying to transform what sounded like fraud into charity, though the school was the beneficiary. They got $50 per hour for him; he got $15 per hour from them.

Also, he hadn't been there long before he suspected that he and the Asian-American and the African-American teachers, both female, comprised the institution's efforts to teach the students about diversity, injecting it into the student body in this small, harmless dose. He overheard some colleagues make veiled, resentful references to affirmative action (since he was blind, both faculty and students often acted as if he were deaf as well), and these complainers kept careful track of their colleagues' pedagogical practices and mistakes.

That he was being used and scrutinized unjustly leached his innocent pleasure in the job. The school profited by his labor, but the personnel subtly encouraged him to feel beholden to his brother-in-law and to the administration for its Christian compassion.

He'd tried to shake off his disenchantment and concentrate on teaching. But tonight, the bitterness surged up like acid reflux as he lay sleepless and weepy in the bed that had come to rest in the wrong room like a boat beached after being adrift. A tsunami of hopelessness crashed over him. His efforts were pointless except as billable hours for the school. He'd wasted his time, his energy.

He'd been the victim of other pranks. He'd opened his lunch sack and unwrapped a tuna sandwich bought at Subway when a peculiar odor like ammonia warned him off. At first, he'd thought the kids at Subway had done something by mistake, then he remembered the lunch sack had sat on his desk while he stepped out for several minutes to the main office. When he'd complained to the vice-principal, she'd just chuckled. "Kids! What was in it, anyway?" Her voice had a grin in it. "I don't know. That's the point. It could be anything. You hear about kids putting drugs in people's food and drink." She said, "Probably nothing. I wouldn't worry about it."

She might worry if she were blind, he thought. He'd gone to her because one of her official duties was to be the disciplinarian.

"They sometimes move the desks when I'm momentarily out of the room."

"Probably just the janitors," she said, with a faint undertone of disdain and irritation. He yearned to thrust his bill of particulars through the bubble of her denial—the sign taped to the back of his blazer that he wore home and didn't discover until he'd hung up his coat and had to wait until his sister came before he could learn that it said "I suck fat ones"; the sensation he had that someone was tracking close behind him as he walked the hall and was gesturing over or about him in a way that puffed slight currents of air on his head. During a tutorial session with a girl about a paper she was writing for an English class, he sensed a good deal of motion around her person near his desk, rustling, shoe-squeaks, little huffs of air bearing scents of sweat and cologne and fruity gum, as if she were engaged in calisthenics while discussing her thesis statement with him. Her voice sounded smirky. Maybe what she was doing was innocent, but the point was he didn't know.

Small humiliations almost every day, though nothing potentially lethal like the tainted sandwich. Three years ago, he'd thought that forcing himself into the world outside this apartment and the familiar paths that he long relied upon to sustain himself would bolster his spirits, restore an equanimity that had been lost to middle-age melancholy. He had blind friends who stayed in good cheer, whose personalities were infused with that can-do spirit, even though they'd had their knocks and bruises in the world. But he'd always had a dark, pessimistic streak, and a tendency to brood in silence about things. The drywall on one bedroom wall had been repaired without his sister's knowledge after he'd put a fist through it. Once, a sighted woman was with him for several months before eventually leaving to take up with an old flame.

He'd said nothing else to the school's official disciplinarian. He'd gotten the message: our parents pay big tuition bucks, so these are bound to be "good" kids.

He'd been aware when that Nedermeyer snot came into the classroom a week ago that something secret transpired between him and Christopher Larkins. People think because you're blind you can't know things by other means. He'd thought of his keys then. Sure enough, they'd been moved. Could've been by accident, but probably not. The kids probably had a copy made, though at the time he'd thought they'd likely copied the classroom key. For the past couple of days he'd been chewing on what to do—surely the school would be alarmed to think that students could come and go as they pleased after hours? He'd been too slow to act, though, partly from a fear that he'd be accused of negligence for letting the keys sit out unprotected. They might think—or even say—that his blindness had caused the trouble, or allowed it to happen, at least. So he'd had to endure this lesson of exactly what the boys had done with the key ring. He hadn't dreamed they'd brazenly crash into his home, scramble his belongings, and injure Millie. Now he burned with shame to realize that his reciting Le Petit Prince had only been a ruse to stall for time.

What a fool!

Helplessness was so infuriating. It provoked a pointless rage that bumped like a wasp against a window. He'd hoped that he'd dampened this lifelong anger, but here it was again pounding at his ribs to be unleashed.

What could he do? The police might find it juvenile but likely not criminal—the kids didn't break down the door or come in a window. Was there a city ordinance against a practical joke that seriously inconvenienced the butt of it? Was it against the law to profoundly dishearten somebody? Can you do jail time for making someone weep from frustration and anger?

Of course, they had apparently injured Millie, and that might indeed be actionable.

He wouldn't complain to his sister, though. She'd nag her husband into forcing the issue at the school and next thing he'd be hearing something like it's probably best if we didn't expose you to these dangers any more. No, he'd just say kids in the building did it and he'd already talked to their parents, and so forth. He'd always been a deliberate person—being blind taught that so he wasn't eager to close out options before he'd considered exactly how to handle this. He yearned to have control, to apply a solution himself. He didn't want the situation wrenched away by well-intentioned parties thinking he was altogether impotent. They might not approve of his solution. Why? Because he wanted justice.

He knew that some might say his rage was disproportionate to the "crime," especially considering these adversaries were officially children. But, he would argue, children in name only. Apparently they had full possession of a motor vehicle and the time, strength and freedom to execute this prank. They'd left school to do it; they had no fear of the school's so-called authorities. They were capable of heaving about heavy pieces of furniture, as capable as most adults. Their half-developed brains with stunted frontal lobes were stuffed with the sorry detritus of popular culture, their language coarse and vulgar, hardly more complex than a trained chimp's base proficiency in ASL. And yet they believed themselves to be superior—to him, to the children of color in surrounding ghettoes who struggled in public schools, even to their own arrogant parents. They were in utter contempt of the other, and since they were ignorant and sheltered, almost everyone else was other.

He had good students, of course—decent, hard-working, well-mannered kids. But these wanna-be gangsters needed to be disciplined. What was possible? Send them to the office for detention?

They'd laugh. Lecturing would be pointless—these miserable cretins had no shame.

God, did he understand those poor young wretches in the Trench Coat Mafia!

"Check this out."

Toby clicked on a file and they watched the clip open and play.

"Dude!" yelled Bradley. "He's groping his fridge."

They all laughed so loud other customers glared up from their laptops and phoess and newspapers and double-whipped foam lattes. They squelched their guffaws and giggled while the clip glided on. Chris thought it was so cool how Toby had milked the files by parking outside Baldwin's building. They'd planted a mini spycam with a 9-volt battery transmitter high on a shelf between two fat books with those raised dots, and it broadcast wireless to Toby's laptop. They were meeting after school now to choose the most hilarious clips to post on YouTube.

The cam got images only from the main room Chris and Bradley had moved the bed to. And they hadn't realized the blind man wouldn't turn on the lights after dark. But they had clear pictures of him coming in the door, slapping the fridge, dropping the cane, standing there like a doofus, and then it looked as if he was talking or yelling.

"What's he saying?" asked Chris.

"Calling for his fucking kitty, I guess," said Toby.

"Did you guys see a cat there?" Chris asked. "I didn't see one."

They played those frames over and over, and every time his mouth opened, they started saying, along with him, "Kitty! Where are you!?" That cracked them up. Thing is, though, it wouldn't be funny to anybody who didn't know he was blind. It would just be a guy standing in his foyer calling out for somebody.

Then he poked the hassock with his cane and bent down to stroke the thing.

"He's getting off, man," Ahmed said.

"Dude has a furniture fetish," said Bradley.

That about wasted them, too.

But really, the footage was a little disappointing. They'd planted the webcam imagining an old-time movie, slapstick stuff, where he'd whack his head on something and bowl over backward, bang his balls on a table corner. Somebody had posted a popular and hilarious YouTube clip that caught an old fart falling down on an escalator, getting up and falling down over and over, and they'd hoped to top that one. But nothing like that happened. For one thing, the teacher was slow and careful. He figured out pretty quickly that everything was changed. It wasn't as good as the clip they'd posted a week or so ago of him yakking on and on about Haley's paper while she flashed her naked tits at him. That one had gotten thousands of hits.

The last clip, in the half dark—some light seeped in from the street, at least—showed him moving about beside his bed, taking off his clothes maybe. Then he seemed to get under the covers. The angle on the bed from the cam was high and from the side—a good one if there'd been more light.

They watched for a moment. Nothing seemed to happen, but just about the time the webcam would've clicked off from inactivity, the covers around the blind man's chest rose and fell, rose and fell.

"Whass up?" asked Ahmed.

They bent closer on their high chairs toward the screen. The picture was frustratingly dim, though that rhythmic movement was visible.

"Hey, he's beating off!" crowed Toby.

"Aw, no way," said Brad.

"Yeah, really. No shit. Check it out!"

They eagerly pushed their faces forward. It might be that. You could decide it was that, if you wanted.

"Yeah, absolutely," declared Toby.

"Fucking hilarious," said Chris.

"Naw," said Brad after a moment. "Too slow."

"He's old."

"No wonder he wasn't at school today."

They laughed. And Baldwin's shoulders kept rocking up, down. Chris squinted hard. Then, to his surprise, he thought he saw the teacher's hands come up out of the covers to press against his face.

"He's like bawling," Chris blurted out.

"No fucking way," said Brad.

They all frowned, lunged forward, peered at the screen as if through a rain-smeared windshield. It was true. Shocked, they watched the teacher lie with his hands over his face and his shoulders shuddering. But when he stopped moving, the webcam clicked off.

They sat transfixed by the blank screen. They didn't look at one another. Chris felt as if everyone in the room stared at them, though they were absolutely silent. Eyes burned the back of his head, and hairs rose on his nape. He gazed down at the table top. "Awwww," said Toby, at last. "Poor baby," he sing-songed. "Somebody moved his beddie-bye!"

They all laughed.

Toby got a call from Haley on his cell and went outside to talk. Although Chris thought maybe Ahmed and Brad would run the clips again, nobody touched the laptop and they hunkered in silence drinking their jacked-up lattes and averting their gazes from even the wallpaper of Britney Spears climbing out of a cab without her panties on.

Chris said, "What if he like finds the webcam?"

"He's blind," scoffed Brad.

"But you know, somebody's bound to come help him put the furniture back. They probably even did that today, and that's why he wasn't in school."

"Okay, so what?"

Ahmed was watching them both, as if waiting to decide which team he'd wind up on. Chris didn't want to go on and on about this, but Baldwin's crying seemed to make this serious, as if the teacher wouldn't just laugh it off. And, okay, it had been rude. Chris hadn't thought of it as something bad, though—it was just funny. The bit with Haley had made them famous at school, but with each wave of higher visibility, Chris had grown more nervous that the news would reach someone in charge. But at least her face didn't show, and he had pretty solid deniability. He'd been a lookout and looked in when she did it, but unfortunately saw only her bare back.

"I dunno," Chris said finally. "The thing would be evidence, you know, a link to us."

"Not to worry. That cam doesn't have any names on it."

Chris turned to Ahmed. "How about your fingerprints?"

Brad brayed at him. "Fingerprints? You think C.S.I. is gonna dust it down and put out an APB on us? Come on! We rearranged the man's furniture! So fucking what?"

When they left, they went out the door singing, "Oooo, kitty where arrrre you?!" to each other.

On the morning following the upheaval of his belongings, Baldwin's sister had brought a mover to help her brother restore order. She'd taken this opportunity to do a thorough cleaning. Wearing a painter's mask to protect her airways from feline dander, she was lifting things from his shelves and dusting them when something odd fell onto the floor. She set it in his hand and said,

"I'm not sure what this is. But I think it's one of those little cameras for computers?"

Shocked, he ran his fingers over it. He had the presence of mind to say, "Ah. Yes. It's something I'm doing to help to research efficiency."

When she left, he sat on his couch cupping it in his hand, trying to imagine what it might have broadcast. The little savages had not only pulled this thoughtless prank, they'd engineered a way to witness his humiliation, revel in it.

He thought long and hard. In the end, he didn't crush it under his heel; he set it back into the shelf. Locating its glassy eye with his finger pad, he pointed it toward the ceiling. A blind camera, useless to them. Perhaps they wouldn't know he'd found it. They couldn't be sure he knew, anyway.

He'd hoped to use subsequent tutoring sessions to slyly ferret out who'd done what (pointless to ask why), but, not really to his surprise, the particular bunch he considered suspects were mysteriously absent from their sessions, with the exception of Christopher Larkins.

He was cool to the young man but took care to be business-like so as not to alert him. In the middle of the session, the boy asked, "Do you mind if I ask something, Mr. Baldwin?"

"I don't know. I'd have to hear what it is. I might mind. I might not, Christopher. What's it about?"

"I was just wondering if you'd ever thought about having a dog."

"A dog?"

"Yes. You know, a seeing-eye dog."

"They're called guide dogs or service dogs."

"Oh."

The teacher checked his normal impulse to answer such a question in a complete way.

"What makes you think I don't?"

"Uh, well, you don't bring one to school."

"True. Why do you want to know?"

The teacher could literally hear the boy's shrugging, the muted, sibilant sss of his shirt sliding across his shoulders. These thugs would kidnap and torture the dog if he had one. It could be they thought he'd gotten one since trespassing into his apartment. "I dunno. Just curious, I guess."

"I see. Well, no. I don't have a guide dog." He had a cat, as they well knew. He had to bite his lip to keep from lunging at the boy and shaking him for what they'd done.

"Are you maybe wondering what it's like to be blind?"

The boy's embarrassment was palpable in the air; a faint heat and a rustle of shifting limbs wafted across the space between them to brush the blind man's face.

"Aw naw. Not really."

Four days after the prank, on a Saturday morning, the blind man found his cat lying motionless with her head and shoulders under the sofa. She was scarcely breathing. He'd noted the evening before that she hadn't eaten much of her Natural Balance Ultra Formula. He called his vet, and she told him to bring Millie in at once, so he put her in the carrier, called a taxi, and arrived at the clinic minutes later. When the vet, a woman who'd been Millie's doctor for three years, examined her, Millie was breathing fast and shallow but otherwise not moving. He told the doctor about the possible injury that might've happened when his furniture was moved. "We'll do an X-ray, but I don't think she has any bones broken or she'd jump or flinch just to be examined. I'm feeling her now to check. Nice kitty. That's a good girl, Millie."

The vet was always thoughtful about remembering that he needed to be told what was happening.

The vet said that Millie should stay overnight for observation and have her blood and urine tested. The blind man went home empty-handed except for his cane. The next morning, a Sunday, the doctor called. Millie had died during the night. The doctor suspected it was cardiomyopathy.

"What's that?" demanded the blind man.

The veterinarian explained that it was a heart condition. She knew from Millie's file that the blind man had rescued her from the streets six years ago when she was already an adult. She'd had heart worms then and they'd treated her for that, but there was no telling how much damage had already been done by that time.

"We're guessing her age to be at least ten. That's old for a cat who had a hard life on the streets as a kitten and young adult," the vet said gently.

"What about her injury? Couldn't it have been from her injury?" he insisted. He ignored the doctor's implication that it was "Millie's time," as a religionist might put it.

The doctor replied that, of course, an injury could be a possible factor. She was thinking of a hypothetical injury such as a heart worm might do, for instance, at any time in the cat's long history. But the blind man heard differently. He now had the choice of believing either that his Millie had died naturally from a heart condition of long standing or believing that her condition had been

65

profoundly aggravated by the injury done to her by the boys. If they were not directly responsible for her death, they had brought it on prematurely.

A dark place inside him began to feed on this interpretation of the doctor's news, as if it had an especially keen appetite for the criminal act, and it grew vigorous and tumescent on the idea of an outrage. It wasn't long before he had remolded the doctor's words so that she was saying Millie's unexpected death had been caused by the injury done to her heart during the boys' reckless deed.

The next morning, a Monday, the blind man stood at the counter of the hardware store.

"What can I do you for, Mr. Baldwin?" He knew this clerk— he lived with his partner in the blind man's building. Nice young man. Always polite and helpful, and not making a production of it, either.

"I have a stopped-up drain."

"Bathroom or kitchen?"

The blind man hesitated. "Sometimes both."

"You wanna plunge or burn? We got a snake, too."

"I have a plunger. It's not doing the job." He chuckled. "And I don't think this calls for the rotor-rooter, yet!"

"Something like Drain It or Liquid Klean, then?"

"Yeah. Whatever's the strongest."

"Actually, we've got something called Works Best that we hear good reports on. It's got a hydrochloric acid base. You wanna be careful with it, though."

The blind man said, "Yes. I wouldn't want to blind myself." The clerk chuckled politely. The joke might've startled him, since the protocol for exchanges with blind persons is to pretend that they are sighted. Or that their blindness isn't visible.

The blind man carried the jug of chemical cleanser home in a plastic bag, walking three blocks from the store to a bus stop. He suspected the boys had used this hardware store to cut the key, as it was only minutes by car from the school. The store wasn't on his usual routes, so securing the right bus at the stop required that he ask someone standing beside him for the number of each approaching bus, and once, when he was standing alone, he had to tap up to the hissing door and shout into the entry, "Is this number thirty-nine?"

But there seemed to be poetic justice in arming himself from this particular store. Holding the container in his lap, he was comforted by its heft. Not that he meant to swing it like a club. The hardware store would send someone out to change his lock and install a safety chain, but, still, now that he knew the full reach of their malice, he'd take no chances.

"Christopher, what in the world are you doing?"

"Nothing."

"Well, watch where you're going, please. I've got all these receipts in order."

Chris opened his eyes. He'd bumped a corner of the dining table and jostled her stacked-up papers. Milk from the glass sloshed onto the heel of his hand. The pb & j sandwich had a sinkhole where his thumb had jammed it to keep it steady.

"Sorry."

He passed through the dining room and into the hall, closing his eyes for the last several feet to the door. He stood with the sandwich between his jaws and felt about for the knob and turned it. He shuffled like a prisoner in chains over the threshold, felt for the desk by the door, eased the milk glass down on it.

He opened his eyes again. The dark grey screen of his Sony begged to be set alight with color, but he ignored it. Blind people can't watch TV. But they have them. A 13-incher sat in Baldwin's shelf below where they'd put the cam. Maybe he listened to programs—talking heads. Maybe visitors used it.

Blind men have beds like everybody else's. They have kitchens, refrigerators. It'd been too dark to see what Baldwin was up to when he returned from the other rooms, but when he got the box running and opened the door, the light in it allowed them to watch him feel around. This thought had come to Chris unexpectedly: the blind man could see better in his apartment with the lights off than they could. He managed to plug in the refrigerator in the dark, but they couldn't see anything at all until he opened the door. He drank right from the milk carton, something Chris did all the time. Then he'd pulled up what looked like an apple and bit from it. No big deal. Too much of what he did made him look like everybody else for it to be funny.

Chris lay in the dark on his bed chewing the sandwich with his eyes closed. The blind teacher had no photographs sitting out, at least none Chris could remember. Baldwin had to rely on pictures in his head, visual memories. Was he blind at birth or was he blinded? What could've made him blind? How would you go to school blind? Did all his textbooks have those raised dots that formed an alphabet? Wikipedia said it was the Braille system, and another link was about the blind using voice recognition and OCR-to-voice software. Braille was weird to think about. Maybe Baldwin would show him a book. Not a bad idea to suck up a little, anyway. Raised dots. Like zits. Waggle your fingers across your forehead—what's it say? Loser! You could go around reading stuff like cheese graters. The driveway had that pebbly concrete, like a huge font to a blind man, saying PARK HERE! Rough sandpaper would like go on and on making the same old gripe. Nail file ditto in a girly voice.

Did Baldwin have a girlfriend? Was she blind, too? That would be very weird. In movies and tv shows, if there's a romance, the blind guys always feel the faces of their lovers with their fingers. Creep you out, really. But, on the other hand, let's say you're blind and you have to "see" Haley's tits with your hands. Poor old Baldwin had them right in front of him and didn't know it. Of course, even though Chris knew they were there he couldn't see them, either, from his post at the door. Might as well have been blind.

Had Baldwin ever been married? What happened to his wife? Did she leave him because he went blind?

He munched on the sandwich. The taste of it seemed stronger, richer, much more peanut-ty eating it with your eyes closed. You could even smell it better.

Just as he was finishing it, he heard a bumping sound at the door, then a jangle. Butkis shoved his snout under Chris's arm.

"It's all gone."

He swung his legs over and sat up. The lab milled on the rug before him, whining, front paws dancing.

"Okay, but you're going to be a guide dog, get it?"

Chris pulled a t-shirt out of his dresser drawer and folded it to tie around his eyes. Blind-folded, he undid the belt to his khakis, slipped the end under the dog's collar and through the buckle loop so that he had a leash. A rack of leashes was screwed to the wall by the back door, but it seemed like cheating to use one.

"Okay, let's go."

The dog was eager to walk, as always. Normally he half-dragged Chris about on their jaunts, and as soon as Chris gripped the end of the belt, the lab lunged for the door. Chris kept up a steady stream of commands that the dog failed utterly to follow. Okay, let's wait here while I close the door. Okay, we're going calmly down the hall because the blind dude you're leading has to make sure he doesn't whack his head. Don't like just barge into the dining room...

"Christopher, I told you—"

"Sorry. We're on our way out."

"What are you up to? Why the blindfold?"

"Experiment for psychology class."

Butkis knew the way to the front door, through it, down the steps and the front walk—the dog knew every foot of their route, of course, but Chris had to yank him back when he tried to tug too fast. Definitely would need training! Chris had one arm before him like a bumper guard as they went, haltingly, half-stumbling onward, but he still slammed into a stop sign pole with his shoulder and wound up with a purple bruise.

"Mister Baldwin, I'm guessing that even if you don't use it, you do understand how the Internet works?"

"Of course."

He'd not had many occasions to be in the principal's office, and he was keenly attuned to how the windows overlooked—or, more properly, underlooked—a construction site where a twenty-story building was going up. Diesel engine thrumming, shouting in Spanish, the beeping alarm of a large vehicle lurching backward. Air currents and the noise told him a window was cracked open a bit. It was stuffy, the room a tad too warm, the air holding the faintest taint of cigarette smoke, though tobacco in any form was prohibited on the campus.

"Are you wanting me to adapt it to my tutoring?"

"Oh, no, no. It's another matter entirely. Let me ask you—do you know of a website called YouTube?"

"Is that the one with amateur videos?"

"Yes."

"I've heard of it."

"Well." The principal paused, and the teacher stiffened. "I'm afraid we have a problem. Some of our students have been posting little films on it. I'm sorry to say that you're the subject of one."

Immediately, the teacher thought of the camera on his shelf, and, electrified by fear and outrage, grit his teeth. What part of his private life was now global property?

"Really? What am I doing?"

"You're not doing anything out of the ordinary. You appear to be talking to one of our students, our girl students, about her paper. You don't seem to be aware that she is, well, not fully clothed while this is going on."

"What?"

"This video was made during a conference. The girl's paper is on Crime and Punishment. She has apparently asked you for help, and the video shows you discussing it while she's... I guess you could say dancing or gesturing in a lewd way." He paused. "Hootchy-kootchy stuff, like." He paused. "Right in front of you."

Something about the sharp inflection at the end of the principal's utterance suggested to the teacher that he'd been caught at this.

"I had no idea!"

His raised voice bounced about the room and he was instantly fearful that he'd protested too much.

"We understand. Do you remember having this conference?"

Of course he did. Was he a moron? But the principal seemed to have a stock of information he was drawing upon and laying out too carefully, piece by piece. Was this an investigation? Was he being interviewed as a, well, person of interest?

"It was about Crime and Punishment, you say?"

"It seems to be."

"Huh. Well, that's not a text I teach. Russian's not among my language skill set. I have been approached now and then to help with various kinds of homework, though."

"You don't recall this student specifically? I'm asking because her face has been blocked out in the video. She must've had someone in the room with her using the camera. We can probably determine her identity by deduction. Junior English is who we have reading that book. And it's a small school."

All this being true, what did they expect of him? The name? He had it clearly in memory, and could even describe his suspicions at the time based on what he'd heard, sensed, smelled. But he balked. He hadn't had sufficient time to absorb this latest outrage to his dignity. He waited, and after a moment, the principal spoke again.

"When it comes to making a determination about the proper disciplinary measure, it's, well, complicated. Parents have a way of getting their backs up when their children are accused of something serious, you know. We would need a witness."

"Am I to be shown a line-up?"

The principal was silent a moment, as if deciding whether to ignore the teacher's sarcasm, then he went on. "Well, we thought you'd recognize her voice or that she'd at least said who she was when she asked you to help."

"She might have. I'll have to think about it." Maybe he was being too cagey, but he wanted time to reflect upon all this before acting.

The principal gave off a muted grunt or sigh that conveyed irritation. And not a little disbelief. "We certainly hope you do. You know, a bad memory in this situation doesn't play well. It's like in court. People get the wrong idea, maybe."

"What do you mean?"

"People would wonder why you wouldn't want to tell all you knew. They might say you knew what she was doing, or even that you'd asked her to do it."

"That's absurd!"

"Like I say, parents can get pretty ferocious."

70

A long silence ensued, long enough that the blind man could track the upward progress of a scaffold across the street as it crawled the side of the skeletal frame, the workers hollering down to partners on the ground as they ascended. Was the principal waiting for him to confess? He seemed to be shuffling papers, the chair creaking as he rotated from one side of the desk to the other.

"You know, we've been pleased to have you here," the principal continued, "even given some of the special arrangements it has required." He sighed, very audibly. "But truthfully, we've got a liability issue. And it seems to me that when our students feel this free to take advantage of you that maybe it'd be best if you went on administrative leave or something for a while."

"Or something?" The blind man couldn't resist aiming this barb across the desk. The pranksters waltz away, the victim is punished!

The principal inhaled, exhaled. "Administrative leave, as I said. Finish out this week, then we can clock your hours down for the next couple of weeks or so. You could stay home, and we'll wait and see how this all shakes out."

"So the school still gets its fifty dollars an hour, right?"

The principal didn't respond; Baldwin heard his words echo in that void and regretted them. He asked, more calmly, "How long, do you think?" even though he was certain the insult had shut this door forever.

"Hard to say. I'll have a little talk with the student and her parents, of course. Most likely others are involved, too." It sounded as if the principal had finished speaking, but then he added, "When and if I find out who they are."

Leaving school that day, the blind man was sure he'd lost the job. The dark place in him pushed aside the possibility that he was being temporarily suspended for his own protection or long-term interests; it quashed any effort to deny the worst. Like the injury to Millie, this too was the fault of those juveniles.

"Interesting that you should ask about that," said Baldwin. "Money. Bringing home the bacon, as they say."

You'd have thought Chris had asked him for his philosophy of life, the way he sat back and rubbed his chin and rocked his head. Chris's question was how could a blind person tell the difference between a one-dollar bill and a twenty. It must be a great mystery or terribly complicated to explain, because the teacher hmmed and frowned, then he reached down into the canvas tote bag he always carried and drew out a Thermos and a big coffee mug.

"Let me wet my whistle here, if you don't mind."

Baldwin was very weird today. Had a freaky little smile, like he knew a secret. Chris had tried to quit French lessons but his step-mom and his dad insisted it was prep for next summer's trip. Then today rumors had been going off like firecrackers that girls were getting called to the office about the YouTube clip. Toby and Brad caught him in gym and said he had to show up for his session today to find out what Baldwin knew.

They'd done twenty minutes of drill from Le Petit Prince, then Baldwin said that part of their lesson was over. To keep from having to do question-and-answer exercises next, Chris asked about the money. It was among a list of things he'd wanted to know.

While Chris waited for an answer, Baldwin carefully set the red Thermos on the desk, unscrewed the lid and laid it aside, top down. He gripped the mug in his left hand, set the bottom of it securely on the desk, then sort of slid the top rim of the Thermos over the mug until it came to rest in a pouring position. Chris felt as if he were watching a demonstration. The teacher then tilted the Thermos gently, cocking his head as if to listen to the liquid move from the one container to the other. A piss-colored stuff, fizzy, with a weird stink, trickled into the mug until he had it about two-thirds full. Maybe it was medicine he took for his condition. Chris would ask about it, but he already had the money question in the air—an earth-shaker, to judge by the build-up here.

"Let me ask you, Christopher. Would you take advantage of a blind man who thought he was giving you a one-dollar bill and he was really giving you a twenty?"

"Probably not."

"Probably, huh."

"Well, no, I wouldn't, I guess. I mean, why would I?"

"Because you could. Because he wouldn't know. Because he'd have no recourse to it. Because he's vulnerable and you're powerful." He paused. "At that moment, I mean."

His pinky touched the rim of the Thermos stopper cap, his hand glided over it, lifted it, brought it over the Thermos and down into the hole. He did it without touching the red canister, like he knew in his head exactly where it was on the desk. He held the Thermos with his left and secured the cap with his right, then lifted the Thermos and leaned over to set it back into the bag.

Then he rose and moved around to the front of the desk, where he eased his hips onto the top, perching himself right in front of Chris's seat on the front row. If Baldwin swung his leg, his brown shoe would kick Chris's knee. The teacher held the mug before his face. Chris thought he'd take a drink now, but he didn't. He sat with it between his palms, index finger crooked through the handle, the way Chris's mom held her tea on cold mornings.

"Although there's a federal case pending on the matter, it might interest you to know that this country is currently the only one on the planet that prints all denominations of bills in the same size and color. If you're blind in any other country, Christopher, you can know what's in your wallet by the size of the bills. I believe you told me recently that your parents are taking you to France next summer?"

"Yeah. Well, Europe."

"Well, if you happen to be blind there, for instance, the hundred-franc note is square, while the five-franc note is rectangular. But that's the old currency. You'll be handling Euros—they increase in size as they increase in value. A neat and simple idea, don't you think?"

Chris would say that Baldwin was staring at him, though of course the teacher was blind. It was the way his face was set so squarely toward his own, though he had to look up at the teacher, who was now looming over him as he leaned. His dark glasses hid what he was thinking or feeling—normally not a matter of curiosity to Chris, but, given all that had happened and the teacher's weird attitude today, everything was up in the air, uncertain.

"Yes," Chris said.

"What we do is fold our bills in a different way according to their value. I leave my ones alone, since they're almost always crumpled or torn. Sometimes they feel limp as thin rags. I fold my twenties in half, and I crimp a corner of my tens, and so forth."

He stopped, smiled from one corner of his mouth. "Does that help answer your question?"

"Uh, yeah."

"These are important lessons, Christopher. Life lessons. Things you might need to know." The teacher raised the mug with both hands and shifted his hands on it slightly, as if he were about to raise it to his lips.

"But that's not the real problem, you see. I can know what bill I've given a clerk, right? But now, think about this. You go to a grocery store and pay for a three-dollar item with a twenty. You're due seventeen dollars change—a ten, a five, a couple of ones, maybe. Or three fives and a couple of ones. Or even seventeen ones, though that's not likely, is it? What if the clerk is thinking, well, this blind idiot can't know what I give him, and I'm making fifteen bucks an hour here and he's probably on welfare. So, I think I'll just give him four ones and tell him it's a ten, a five, and two ones. What do you think, Christopher? What's to stop the clerk from that?"

Chris didn't know he was supposed to answer, and when he failed to, the teacher insisted, "Tell me that. What's to stop him?"

"Nothing, I guess."

The teacher beamed. "Yes, the boy says nothing! The boy can't even imagine what might stop somebody from it! If this mysterious force existed, this thing once called 'common decency,' it would stop someone from pissing on the man's sandwich or putting a vulgar sign on his back, am I right? It would prevent someone from humiliating him by dancing nude in front of him without his knowledge, right? Or it would stop them from breaking into his apartment and rearranging the furniture so that he might trip over it and maybe injure himself. It would stop them from killing his pet! And stop them from planting a camera there so that they could enjoy seeing, peering, watching, spying, observing—you choose your own vision verb here, Christopher, you're the sighted one, I'm the blind one—gawking! Yes, that's the one. Gawking at him!"

The mug between his hands seemed to be quivering, rising, over Chris's head. If the teacher didn't watch out, he was going to spill it.

"Mr. Baldwin, I—"

"Nothing stops them! Nothing! Do you want to know what it's like to be blind? Do you?"

The teacher was trembling. Chris sat paralyzed, staring into the man's navy-blue opaque lenses.

"Hold out your hand!"

Chris slowly raised his arm; the teacher dropped his own right hand from the mug and pawed the air between them, found Chris's wrist and clamped it in his strong hand. The teacher loomed over him, the mug between them close enough to Chris's face that he could see the liquid sloshing. He knew then it was something that could harm him.

"I asked do you want to know what it is to be blind?"

"No sir! Please, Mister Baldwin!"

For a long moment, the teacher gripped Chris's wrist so hard his hand was going numb. The brandished mug might as well have been a gun. The boy, wide-eyed, held his breath.

Then the teacher released and dropped his wrist and slumped back on the desk.

"Go. The lesson's over."

When Chris was safe in the hall, he glanced back through the window in the door then ran on. Still at the desk, the teacher held the mug before him, high and away from his body, like a chalice.

Leave Me Be!

Bobadilla, Spain.

Mother Bradley—

I wish you could see the look on your son's face. Jake's glaring nails out the window as our train goes off to Madrid without me. My uncle would say he looks like he's crapping a brick. (Sorry—I know such expressions make you cringe.) I have no idea how he'll explain why we came back on different flights. Do you know how hard it is for him to be honest with everyone in your family? For instance, when he told you ten years ago that I "miscarried"?

But if you ask me, & I know you will because you could never keep your nose out of our business—Oh my god it feels so good to say that!—I'll tell you it's because of the woman in Granada.

First thing I noticed was she didn't mind the stink of cat pee. Jake & I were picnicking in the courtyard of the Alhambra, & there were I'd say a hundred stray cats begging scraps, mewling & swarming around our legs like floodwater. Jake kept griping about the stench, & of course he didn't want me to feed them, so to get away from the odor we moved closer to the walls that overlook the town. But the woman sat on that bench right in the middle of the courtyard and ignored it.

She was large, about my age—her hair more gray than mine, though—& she was wearing a calf-length rayon dress. It had a white background & red polka-dots the size of cherry Lifesavers (I'd never have had the courage to wear something that bold in a foreign country) & scuffed black pumps with a low heel. I watched her while we sat & ate what we'd bought on the hike up the hill to the castle—cheese & bread and those "blood" oranges that Jake hates because they're the wrong color inside – I swear to God you should be shot for making him such a picky eater! I thought it was fine as a picnic, even if we weren't having your famous German potato salad that Jake always whines about my not making as well as you can, which of course I could easily do if you would ever give me the real recipe! I'd wanted a bottle of red wine, too, but he nixed it because his stomach's been upset ever since we got on the plane at DFW. Naturally.

The woman had a sketch pad & a box of colored pencils on the bench beside her & she was working fast with her right hand— the pad was laid on her left knee which was crossed over her right, & she kept looking from it to the walls & houses down the hill & I will say that they were pretty in the sunlight, all pastels like Easter dresses. Now & then she reached quick into the box to pluck a particular color without fumbling, as if she knew just where each was, sure as a harpist. A pair of plastic ear clips as round & red as the polka-dots lay on the bench beside her. She had on a big straw hat more to keep the sun off than for fashion because the purple ribbon on it didn't go with her dress (but the shoes didn't work, either, to my mind—you'd have worn white and I red ones), but, anyway, as usual, I forgot & made the mistake of asking, "Jake, what country do you think that woman comes from?"

It just popped out. It was the dress. American women usually wear Nikes or Reeboks like mine or sneakers & jeans or sweat suits, slacks or shorts, blouses and sweaters and wind-breakers. I thought maybe she was English; she had that pale skin & big horse teeth & a beaky nose that I associate with women from England, mostly from watching Masterpiece Theatre, & those ugly black shoes, too. Oh, & a white cardigan sweater caped across her shoulders! She was a teacher on vacation, maybe. An old maid. Anyway, I should have known better than to ask Jake about her. He hates this kind of thing. If we're down at El Patio on Thursday night for the all-you-can-eat buffet & somebody I don't know comes in, my mind goes to work on them. A few weeks ago there was this threesome—a young man in his late 30s in gray slacks & a navy blazer who might've just come from behind his teller's window & a young woman Lauren's age or maybe still in school in designer jeans & a tweed jacket & an older woman with frosted hair & several rings including a diamond that winked at me from across the room, who was in a mocha-colored Jones of New York silk suit. Mother, son, & granddaughter? I wondered, but then the girl kept reaching for the man's hand & playing with it so I knew she & the fellow were a new couple, & I'd have bet a dollar to a doughnut that this was the first meeting for the soon-to-be second wife and her soon-to-be mother-in-law. And she'd be formidable, don't you know? Like maybe she had money & didn't mind one bit hearing her children have to wheedle it out of her. And I don't know why, I had this picture of Jake with a new young woman who had no idea poor thing what she might be getting into. And I just knew that this was the first all-you-can-eat Tex-Mex buffet for that mother-in-law, too. If she ate at a restaurant you can bet it had valet parking. She was the kind to eat fried chicken with a knife & fork, when she had to eat it at all.

I don't know why I'm going on & on about that woman. Anyway, I asked Jake did he think that trio was a couple out with the young man's mother.

He snorted & said, "Damned if I know! Why don't you go ask them?"

I don't know why it makes him so mad to hear me guess about these things, but I said, "Well, I don't need to know for sure."

"Then what's the point, Kathy?"

"I just wanted to know what you think."

"How can I think anything about total strangers?"

He had chili gravy on his chin but I wasn't about to tell him. I was tempted to say the older woman reminded me of you, but then I realized he wouldn't bother to ask me in what way. He was busy adding up the bill on his calculator, which annoyed me no end. I mean, it's always $12.99 each plus $2.50 for tea & 8.25% for tax, unless he has a beer too & I just kept my mouth shut & got out a dollar from my purse to leave for the bus boy because Jake won't tip if you have to serve yourself at a buffet, & I know he didn't learn that from his father!

So, when I asked what country he thought the artist in the polka-dotted dress was from, he said, "Mongolia."

"I think England," I told him. It was nice of me to ignore his mockery, I believe.

"Think what you want."

"I will!" I said.

You can probably tell we were testy. We've been traveling three weeks solid, &, as you well know, he didn't want to include Spain. Far as he was concerned, we could spend the whole time in Scotland or England so he could play golf & wouldn't have to strain his brain figuring out how to tell a waiter he wanted whatever form of beef the nation might be serving. He's not been happy with any meal so far, & while I suppose that flatters me, I've been content with everything that's been set before me because I didn't have to make it. He gripes & I gripe about his griping. Now I know why we've waited decades to come over here. It's gotten to where I sit down with a stomachache before I've eaten a bite. Four days ago in Paris, a gypsy child tried to yank his wallet from his pocket while we were standing outside Sacre Coeur cathedral, & he went ballistic as Lauren would say & would've broken that child's arms if he'd caught up with him. He wanted to spend the day at the police station reporting this, but I wanted him to laugh it off so we could enjoy our scheduled lunch-time barge tour of the Seine. He gave in but glowered all afternoon & was even mad at me for "taking the kid's side." Next day I wanted to see the Impressionists at the

Musee d'Orsay & he wanted to visit the Eiffel Tower, which I had no interest in, but when I suggested that he go there while I was at the museum, you should've heard him squawk! So instead he dogged my heels all through the museum & kept sighing & looking at his watch & finally I snapped & told him to wait for me in the cafeteria. They say that you're supposed to have one hour away from your companion for each day of travel, but he's never been one to spend a minute alone unless it's television or a newspaper. Being together day in day out has made me realize how much we avoid one another at home. I'm always asleep or faking it when he gets up at 6 & goes to your house for breakfast, and he doesn't get home until after six in the evenings & wants an hour to read the paper and have his Jack Daniels & water before dinner, so by the time I've put it on the table we might have thirty minutes to talk before something comes on television one of us wants to see, & then next thing you know I'm cleaning up the kitchen & getting myself groomed for sleeping.

Ironic—at home I have endless hours to myself, hours I use in ways he's not curious about. At dinner he never asks me what I've done during the day—I have to volunteer it. But over here he's not let me have a minute to myself. I did manage to get "lost" one afternoon in Paris—snuck out of the hotel while he was napping—& spent three delicious hours alone strolling in the Left Bank imagining that I was a young student in a black leather jacket & long, stringy hair & a pack of strong cigarettes & a big cup of rich coffee on my table at an al fresco café, sitting across from a fellow in similar garb & a guitar to boot, who's known me only long enough to still want to impress me. I'll admit to wishing I hadn't married so young. What I did about all that was buy a big bar of Toblerone white chocolate and I ate on it nonstop until I felt sick.

When I got back he was frantic with worry. (Okay, I admit that was a little gratifying, and yes, Margaret, I know I should've left a note.) He made me swear never to go out alone again. It's as if an Arab or such will kidnap & sell me into white slavery. (I doubt I'd inspire high bidding on the block!) Of course, if I asked him if that's what he's scared of, he'd deny it. (But, of course, if he asked me what I thought of being kidnapped by an oil-rich sheik, I'd lie.) We've been getting on each other's nerves is what I mean.

At the Alhambra courtyard, his snide remark about "Mongolia" annoyed me. I needed a minute to myself, so I said, "I'm going to go find some water," & he said, "No, you stay here. I'll go." And he walked off toward the palace. (Renaissance, built by Charles V, just so you won't think we wasted all our time squabbling.) I wanted to ask if he thought I was safer here than walking around the grounds, but then my guess was that he went because he wanted to be the one to say who stayed. It was my lot to tend our sorry little stinking hearth & his to go off hunting & gathering.

Either way, it was good to get him out of my sight. I watched the woman for a while. The flies in the courtyard were bad but she just jerked her head when one landed on her cheek or flicked at them with her fingers. I was dying to walk around behind her to see if what she'd done was any good—I'm that way when I see an artist working in public. But I didn't want to intrude. I admit I wanted to strike up a conversation for reasons that aren't becoming: I probably wanted to have her pleasure rub off on me by talking to her or maybe I wanted to spoil her fun out of envy. Like at Lauren's wedding when I know that I looked especially nice in that smart-looking linen suit that I'd searched for months to buy. I was determined that the MOB wasn't going to look like a scoop of melting sherbet. The particular shade of green nicely set off my hair & skin, I think —& of course I knew it wasn't just my imagination because when you saw me in the church foyer as we were lining up to go in, you said, "I could have loaned you my pearls to go with that if you'd only asked," while you squinted at my coral necklace, which I know you thought was too, well, "fun" for the mother-of-the-bride, but it was one of the few pieces of jewelry your son ever gave me unprompted & picked out completely by himself (so far as I know) on a business trip to Phoenix, where I guess he did something to atone for. (And BTW—the verb form is "to lend," not "to loan.")

So, point is, if I'd spoken to the woman I wouldn't have had her welfare in mind. So, instead, I sat & indulged this peculiar hobby. She had an interesting habit of licking the pad of her index finger then rubbing a spot on the paper with it, quickly & lightly. At first I thought she did it to erase something, then I guessed that it made a washing effect. Her leg swung a little, not so much to joggle her pad, just her body soaking up the motion of her hand & arm & the dip & weave of her head as her gaze went up & down. She was completely wrapped up in it. You could've yelled her lottery number in her ear & she'd have never heard it. She never stopped once to stretch, yawn, or look around. I wondered where else she'd been & if she'd come to Granada before. Was she a widow? She didn't seem like all those poor widows (no offense!) you see on the tour buses— row after row of small grey heads with the backs of the seats standing over them a little like tombstones. I mean, I think this woman was content to travel and be alone. She was... I can't find the right word. She would go off & have her dinner when she felt like it, have it just where she wanted to eat, have what she wanted without defending her choice or justifying the expense; then she'd go out to a movie or anywhere she liked & stay as long as she wanted without having to apologize or explain.

I was having so many ideas about her that I almost wished Jake would hurry back so I could describe them to him, even though I knew my thoughts would only irritate him.

I planned the rest of her trip. I imagined the announcer on "Wheel Of Fortune" describing that new travel package on the wheel—You'll go on from here to Barcelona & to the Riviera, where you'll tan topless on the sand at Cannes, your big old droopies just hanging there but you won't give a darn—they don't want to see 'em, they don't have to look, is what you'll think!

At Monaco she'll wait in the palace courtyard for hours hoping to see Ranier or one of Princess Grace's children, wait until she's tired of it, then she'll go to a casino & plop down every penny of her nest-egg & not get up from the roulette table until she's blown it all if she so chooses, or she'll sit & feed quarters to the slot machines all night & not have to hear some fellow in Cole-Haan loafers he bought for himself criticize her for it! She'll sit at the bar alone drinking something dangerously potent & wait for an oil-rich sheik to kidnap her. She will order room service without glancing at the prices. She will amble down the street in Rome & when she wants a cigarette she will ask a strange man for one.

Self-contained, that's the word.

Or maybe this is last stop before her thatched cottage a couple hours out of London in a village she's lived at forty years. A Corgi, English bone china, shelves full of knick-knacks she's collected world-over without getting anyone's consent & murder mysteries open face-down on tables everywhere. Unfinished jigsaw puzzles, sewing projects abandoned undone right there in the seat of a chair. For weeks! There's a fireplace with two small chintz wing-chairs & little hassocks with needlepoint covers & hand-knitted Afghans for when her sister or a friend comes to visit. She won't worry about lunch until she gets hungry then she'll eat a can—she'll call it a "tin" I believe—of beets & soda crackers & be perfectly content with it. Later she'll stroll down the lane with the dog.

I wondered what she'd say if I offered to trade lives sight unseen? Would there be something about hers I was overlooking? Was she ever lonely? Would she envy me my husband? The label "old maid" had come to mind automatically. When Jake & I were in high school, we always called our single women teachers "old maids" if we didn't like them, but, you know, most weren't yet thirty. Girls Lauren's generation would never call a single woman that. And there's been so much in the press these past few years about women coming into their own after their children leave home & they've been through menopause—starting businesses, writing books, going back to school, having first careers at last or changing to new ones, climbing Everest or going to an ashram in India. *Eat Pray Love.* Just out & out re-inventing themselves, I guess you could say —that it makes me annoyed with myself for not having done more with my life or at least have used the three years at UT in some way. It was far too big a strain on my parents for me to go there, but, of course, my mother always believed it accomplished its true purpose. And it seems downright ungrateful to whine about it, seeing as I've spent the last thirty-one years in comfort without lifting a finger to provide for myself or my children. It was what we were taught to want, especially if your mother had to take in ironing. I can't fault it much as a system without feeling foolish or hypocritical for enjoying the benefits. My husband, your son, our Jake, has gone off to work every weekday of the past thirty years without complaint, & once he got out of law school & we paid back his loans —there, well, I did forget about having to wait tables at Denny's for a spell, probably wanted to forget it & all the similar jobs I had in high school!—we've had nothing but good fortune since & if he's cornered his secretaries in the coat closet or bought the comfort of a prostitute on an out-of-town trip, it hasn't inspired him to leave me. Yet. And I'm counting on the community-property laws of the state of Texas to protect me if he does.

I'm rambling. I'm trying to explain why I didn't get on the train to Madrid, trying to explain why I seemed to envy a homely Englishwoman wearing a dress I wouldn't be caught dead in who was sketching happily at the Alhambra all by herself. I mean I seemed to have finally noticed my problem then, though I have to ask why was I blind for so long? Because it was comfortable? I thought maybe we'd worn ourselves thin being together day in, day out, so different from being at home where we've worked out ways of being apart without even knowing it. I meant worn ourselves thin temporarily, on this trip, but now I'm not sure if I don't mean year in, year out.

Jake came back with a newspaper and a bottle of water, complaining about what it cost. I kept staring at the Englishwoman, trying to get Jake to notice my interest in her.

He said, "You're so curious, did you ask her where she's from?"

"No."

"I guess you'd rather make it all up in your head than find out what's real," he said.

That made me a little mad. He's a big one for what's "real," or at least he thinks so, until it comes to things he doesn't want to know, such as that his son doesn't really want to be in law school & has a secret wish to be a forest ranger. Or that his own daughter, your granddaughter, is most likely a lesbian who married to hide it from him & maybe from herself. (When her roommate called drunk & sobbing the night before Lauren got married & poured out her soul to me, he said, "That girl always did seem wacko," and he meant the roommate. But I've seen them together, felt the undercurrents. And that snapshot tucked into the girl's mirror, them at a party embracing & kissing on the mouth that way. Of course, I would never ask & I didn't say a word about that call to her no matter how much it worries me. And I trust you won't, either.)

Margaret, I doubt he knows that he no longer loves me. He's such a "realist" that acknowledging the truth would require him to do something about it, about me, about the rutted hum-drum of our life. Me, I can see whatever & not feel compelled to act accordingly. A lifetime of adapting to someone else's priorities has taught me that. So, yes, I'd rather "make it up all in my head" as he puts it, than go "find out what's real."

I stewed for a bit, then I said, "Do you think she's happy?" meaning the artist.

He smiled at my question. "She's not whistling."

I wanted to ask are you happy? But I was afraid of what he'd say. I wanted him to ask me was I happy. I'd have told him I felt like jumping off the Eiffel Tower. I can't explain why. If I was still having periods, I could blame it on that.

I said, "No, but she looks so engrossed in what she's doing."

"That's true."

"What do you do that makes you feel that way?"

Jake gave me a strange look. It was a question you might ask on your third or fourth date, if the first few have gone well, or you'd ask it on the first date if the person was the one you wound up being with all your life. I probably could've answered it for him, but I think I was trying to uncover anything new in him. Or maybe I was trying to rekindle my interest in him & his in me, or ours in us—this is hard to explain!—you know, come at the same-old from a new tack, the way when you go the opposite way on a street you've only traveled one way for years you're amazed to see that dry cleaners you had no idea was there.

"Well, work sometimes, it makes me feel that way." He squinted at me, as if I'd changed into someone else. "You know that. Don't you?"

"What about it? When? I mean." Since I was annoyed with him, I hated to sound like I was interviewing a fascinating world figure I couldn't get enough of.

He shrugged. "If I have a case & I'm trying to imagine the circumstances that might have led to an action, build a scenario, I can get pretty wrapped up in that."

"Aha! Making up stuff!"

"All in the service of the client. I can charge two hundred & seventy-five dollars an hour for it."

Oh, I hated that answer! My imaginings were worthless, literally. "Any other times?" I'm afraid my voice might have sounded too pleading.

"Well, playing golf, of course. I lose track of time out there; everything fades away." He frowned; he was puzzled. "I've told you before."

"How about sex?"

"Sex?"

"Does it make you happy?"

"It's good, all right."

His answer didn't fit my question. He saw me look at the artist.

"Is that what she's having?" he asked with a grin.

"Yes," I said, "I'll have what she's having."

Jake laughed. I'm good for something, it seems.

Then, a surprising thing happened: as we were watching, this fellow walked up from out of nowhere. He had Albert Einstein hair & tortoise-shelled glasses, rumpled tobacco-colored corduroys & a baggy herringbone tweed coat with leather elbow patches. He was carrying a paperback in one hand with his thumb jammed into it the way you do when you stop reading to do something else but plan to get right back to it, & in his other hand was a glass of red wine. When the man approached her, I was a little alarmed. She'd created a force field about her person with her intense concentration, & I couldn't imagine stepping through it myself. My thought was that this was a quaint meeting of two English eccentrics in a foreign place, &, seeing that she was apparently alone & perhaps a fellow countryman, maybe he presumed he could intrude. Jake was sneakily watching them over the edge of the USA Today.

The man set the glass beside the woman as if she'd ordered it—they were together.

"Do you need anything else?" the fellow asked in an accent posh as Lord Grantham's.

She shook her head without looking up. "No thank you," she replied, sounding for all the world like Diana Rigg. "Just leave me be. I'm having an experience."

He nodded & turned to go, but, before he walked off, he picked up those red ear clips from the bench & slipped them into his jacket pocket!

I watched him stroll off about fifty yards & ease down onto another bench next to a wicker picnic hamper. I suppose he'd been there all along & I hadn't noticed him. He picked right up with his reading. You know, he didn't act the slightest bit injured.

The woman went on sketching. I don't think she knew that glass of wine stood not six inches from her elbow or that he'd taken her ear clips.

"What in the world do you suppose she meant by having an experience?" Jake asked me, half whispering.

I whipped my head around, surprised, but, of course, he was only making fun of me.

"I don't know," I said, partly to sulk & partly because I really didn't know.

"You won't even speculate?"

"She meant she was enjoying herself with her art work & didn't want him to spoil it."

"How could he spoil it?"

"By talking to her."

"Boy, that's sure not your cup of tea, is it?"

I couldn't answer, because that was true & it was not true & it would have taken me days to explain the difference, explain it to a man who has lived with me for over thirty years & still knows so little. I felt a pout dropping over me like a net. I tried to radiate my displeasure so he could feel the chill. I had already tidied up from our picnic to keep the cats away, so I got up & slung the knapsack over my shoulder. Without a word, I strode out of the courtyard & into the street that led down the hill toward the city. Margaret, you know I'm not normally the kind to stop speaking & pout. (Am I?) But I had no answer that he would really hear.

Of course, then he came running up behind me, not so much worried about having offended me as afraid a Spaniard might pinch my butt and thereby insult his honor.

"What's the matter?" he whined. "I was trying to talk with you about your mystery woman."

"No, you weren't. You wanted to make a fool of me."

"I can't win!"

There was no point in arguing. Because, you see, he missed all the other, much more important things in that tableau. I wonder if you would've seen them, Margaret—you spent most of your life with a man who never once so far as I know brought you something from the refrigerator when he was rummaging about in it for himself. Don't get me wrong—no, heck, get me as wrong as you want! What do I care!??—Ben was a decent man, but he never gave you a birthday present that couldn't have gone to any female—a dozen red roses, a gold necklace, a box of milk chocolates even though I know you like dark, etc.,—& didn't that ever make you want to scream?

I decided to do what I could. I asked, "Did you see him take her ear clips?"

"Is that what those were?"

"Yes. Why'd he take those?"

We were going down a steep cobblestoned street & I was glad I was wearing sneakers and that the pavement was dry else I'd have to take his arm. Jake was still right behind me, which wasn't usual. He normally walked four or five steps ahead, parting the waves of molesters, or trying to hurry me along. Or trying to run away slow.

"I have no idea."

I guess if somebody were paying him two hundred & seventy-five dollars an hour, he'd try to figure it out! "Why'd he bring her that wine?" I asked.

"I suppose she asked for it."

"Did you hear her ask for it?"

"No, but I wasn't there the whole time, remember?"

"Did she drink any?"

"Why are you on my case about this all of a sudden?"

"I don't know!" I was fairly blubbering by now & could hardly see where my feet were falling.

"Good God, Kathy!" Jake yelled. "What in the world's the matter with you?!"

I could see his patience had worn thin, & I was suspicious that maybe I was acting up to get attention or maybe only to arouse any sort of passion in him. So I got myself under control & stayed that way until this afternoon, but keeping myself reined in was like how when you're nauseated with the flu & you're in public & you put yourself on auto-pilot & stride fast as you can for the nearest bathroom, hoping you can make it through the door before it all lets go. I don't know where the "door" was in this case, I mean the place where I would feel free to let go.

This morning we were cross from the minute we got up. We bickered for thirty minutes over what to do about breakfast, & the upshot was that I ate a leftover orange & some cookies & Jake decided not to eat at all & so could work himself into a real lather. I offered him half the orange. He cursed the Spanish for not having the sense to invent breakfast or at least borrow it from the English or the Germans. Since we'd been in Spain a week already and he'd encountered the same situation each morning and still hadn't thought ahead about it, I believed he was really criticizing me for not solving it for him. I told him I was sure when we got back home you'd have your usual cardiac clogger waiting for him every morning.

By the time we got onto the train we weren't speaking. It wasn't unusual for us to have little to say; this was that silence when you have already said too much. We weren't thirty minutes underway before the train stopped & the most astonishing couple came down the aisle & sat right across & up one row from us. They looked Austrian or German to me—they had matching Tyrolean hats in a hunter-green felt, though hers had a pheasant feather cocked all jaunty in the band—faces like milk cows, really, hers a little paler, but both with the same plump soft cheeks like maybe they'd eaten the same darn lardy thing bite for bite for fifty years. And here's the oddest thing—both were wearing vested suits that looked to have been cut from the same bolt of brown plaid cloth, though hers had a skirt & not trousers. They were probably husband & wife, but I also wondered if they were twins who'd dressed alike for a special occasion such as their birthday. You'd never see a couple in the U.S. in such a get-up. Two people might wear "I'm With Stupid" t-shirts or matching Dallas Cowboys sweats, but not two plaid vested suits! It was a strange sight.

I was on the verge of commenting to Jake before I caught myself. I wasn't about to invite Jake's ridicule by saying word one about them. So far as he might know, I was a person who took absolutely no interest in my surroundings.

"Most ridiculous thing I've ever seen," he muttered.

"What is?" I asked, all innocence.

He tipped his head their way. "Maggie & Jiggs."

This was his way of trying to call a truce & to open negotiations. This, instead of apologizing for yelling at me this morning because the Spanish don't believe in an English breakfast. Sure, it was nice to get this concession, but his tone was so nasty & contemptful that it took me aback. That's not how I play my game.

But to give him the benefit of the doubt, I wondered if it was possible he'd actually missed my speculating, that he'd rather hear me chattering about nothing than be silent, and he was trying to jump-start me. I saw I had a chance to punish him if that was so, but my desire to do that didn't last long.

"I think they look cute," I said, though to be perfectly honest that wasn't exactly what I thought, and you can tell him I said so. "Maybe more couples ought to do that."

Jake sneered. "You want to wear my suits, fine. But you're not getting me into a dress."

I don't know how he got the idea I was prescribing that!

"I don't want you to wear my dresses," I told him. "That's not what I meant at all." My chin was quivering. I admit, I'm a mess these days.

"Why don't you say what you mean, then?" he said.

Oh, gosh! I thought. If we start doing that, we'll be in big trouble!

"Why should I? You never do!" I said.

"What do you mean by that?"

The Austrians, hearing us, glanced over then looked away. The man passed the woman part of a newspaper he was reading. I laid my head back against the seat & closed my eyes so no one could see them.

"Oh great!" Jake said. "A hormone storm! That'll be a big help!"

Hormone storm!!? I was furious, but I bit my lip because I didn't want to make a scene. Pretty soon we stopped here at Bobadilla, where we had to change for the train from Malaga to Madrid. There's no town, just a valley with two sets of railroad tracks & a station between. I sat down with our bags & Jake went off to buy himself something to eat.

When it was time to board for Madrid, I got up & started toward the train with Jake, but when I saw he was going to stay four or five steps ahead of me like always, I stopped right in my tracks.

"Goodbye!" I blurted out. Maybe he heard me, maybe he didn't. Maybe he was pretending he didn't. And maybe it was childish, Margaret. I don't know myself how to judge it. I've got a whole buzzing beehive of maybes swarming around my head right now. All I know is I'm in a mood to have a really BIG "hormone storm," one that sweeps like a tidal wave and drowns everything that breathes or like an earthquake brings the whole darn world down around your ears!

I plopped down onto a bench. He was all the way aboard the train before he had to acknowledge I wasn't following. He came back down the little stairs & yelled, "Come on, Kathy!"

When I didn't answer he saw I didn't want to be called like a dog, so he strode over to within putting distance & stood with his fists on his hips & said, "Come on, now, we'll miss the train. Don't be silly."

"You go on," I said. I couldn't even look at him.

"All right, I will," he said, like it was a threat. "You better—"

"Oh just leave me be!" I yelled. People all around looked at us.

"You got it, sister!" he said.

He got on & came to the window of a compartment & beckoned to me & lip-synced "Come on!" but I ignored him. Then he sat down & pretended to be reading his paper. I could see the top half of his head. When the train jerked and started rolling forward, he jumped up like he couldn't believe it and stared out the window at me with his jaw hanging open.

There's a stir all around me now because another train's coming in. I have no earthly idea where it's going. I need to stop writing & take stock, inventory my overnight bag, Margaret. I've feel like I've survived a shipwreck & just woke up on the beach & have to look about to see what washed in with me that could be used.

But before I run out of steam & lose my courage & decide that this is just a silly snit & Jake never did anything wrong to deserve being married to such a petty neurotic bitch, I want you to know I chose you to hear all this because as much as I hate to think this, I also hate to say it even more, but, you know—we're just alike. And isn't that sad?!

So, Margaret, if you get this, you'll have all my side of the story I can tell at the moment. If I don't come back soon, give Rob that damned Suburban Jake thinks I have to drive. I know you'll feel sorry for Jake when Texas-OU weekend comes around & his old fraternity brothers & their current partners arrive to burn holes in my carpets, so I'll tell you right now that the recipe—the real recipe —for the seven-layer guacamole & bean dip they all like so much is nowhere in the house: it's in my head, & that's where it's staying!

Love,
Kathy

Costume Jewelry

The vase Claude picked up at the Fair Park flea market had a green glaze and was roughly the size and shape of a bowling pin. He wasn't a collector, but he'd watched Antiques Road Show over his wife's shoulder enough to be hooked on turning a tidy profit for little effort. He paid only five bucks, so if it was worth less, no great loss. Jacey was on the far side of the hall with her pal Wendy looking at quilts, so he decided to present it to her only after he'd determined its value.

Alone in his shop behind the garage, he shucked the newspaper wrapping from the vase and set it on his workbench. He dusted off the rounded shoulder with his fingertips. A voice arose suddenly from its pouting, thick-lipped mouth.

"Hello, you've reached Genies Universal, Incorporated! Para Español, toca tres veces. All our representatives are busy at this time. Please select from the following menu: If you've never made a wish, rub your vase one time. If you have questions about your wish, rub it twice. If you wish to speak to a representative, please rub three times then continue holding. This call may be monitored for quality assurance. Thank you for your patience!"

Up swelled banjo music backed by minstrel singers. Claude, startled, lowered the vase and wanted to jerk back his hands and step away, but he didn't from fear it might flail about like a loose fire hose and rap his noggin. Cautiously, he edged closer and peered into its dark interior without fully exposing his face. At a sudden flicker inside, he flinched. Something was moving! A rat stirring from a nap? That was alarming.

But then—

"Hello, my name is Sybil! What is your wish?" The soothing voice reminded him of the On Star muse in his Silverado. It lured him to ease his face over the mouth again. Maybe it was his imagination, but there seemed to be a miniscule female standing on the bottom.

"My wish?"

"Yes, Mr. Lokey. I'll be your genie for today, and I'm authorized to grant you a single wish."

"You are?"

"Yes," said Sybil, with a faint note of impatience.

"What do I wish for?"

"Oh, that's entirely up to you!"

His brain spun. He shook his head like a dog shedding water. But even if this were a hallucination, it would do no harm to wish.

"Uh, like a big wish or just a little one?"

"Up to you, sir." Claude heard a muted tick tick tick, as of tiny fingernails drumming on a ceramic wall.

"Aren't there supposed to be three?"

"Oh, ha ha! You wish!" Sybil chortled. "Those were the golden days, weren't they? No, sir, I'm sorry—just one."

An Audi A4, fifteen-pound weight loss, Cowboys season tickets, free lawn maintenance for a year, George Clooney's hair, to be forty again, a painting contractor you could count on... the list was about to unfurl forth like an ancient scroll, but he recalled the vase was meant to be Jacey's. He'd better add items for her benefit. The thought flit through his head that the wish itself might be hers, but he swatted it down before it could pester him.

"Do I have to make it right this minute?"

"Well, no. You can take some time. Only thing is, we're on a kind of use-it-or-lose-it arrangement. Lotta folks scrabbling for their turn, you know."

"Can I at least have twenty-four hours?" Claude heard a muted whisk, as if a miniature cuff were shoved back to disclose a tiny watch.

"We could do that."

Then the vase was empty. No poof! of genie-dust, no abracadabra smoke, no cartoonish ka-whoosh! like Voyager bolting off at warp speed.

He upended it, shook it, though not without a fear he'd injure the genie or dump out a nasty surprise. Nothing. He set it upright and puffed a breath into it. There was a faint whoo like a note from a blown conch. Had he imagined the wish? Must have. He felt very foolish.

Nonetheless, he pulled his stool up to the workbench, took down his clipboard used for doodling designs for household projects. What could pretending hurt?

New table saw

Hand-held GPS device

72" TV

new iPhone

Oh, come on!

A night with... Well, he only had one night, probably, so who? Julianna Margulies? Julianne Moore? Juliet Binoche? Julia Roberts? Julie Christie or Juliette Lewis? How could a guy choose?

Would having them all bend the rules? Would that dilute his pleasure? Would he be up to such a grand undertaking? And does Jacey find out? Is it serially or concurrent? Could this take place in the Caribbean? More than one night? After all, he'd imposed the limit himself without thinking.

He now understood the need for choice #2 in GUI's voice mail menu.

He put his hand on the vase to stroke it then decided better. Sybil might not appreciate being roused from sleep or ripped away from another client to answer his questions. Though in his own defense, he could point out that no FAQ was offered. It did seem sensible to mull this over rather than yank the genie's chain every time something popped to mind. Maybe, too, there was a genie tech support for people having trouble with their wish.

On his way across the yard, old saws rushed unbidden to mind: wish in one hand, crap in the other; see which fills up the quickest. And If wishes were horses, beggars could ride. Then, just as he reached the door to the kitchen, the most common, the most dire cautionary cliché swung into the air before his eyes like a throbbing neon sign: Be Careful What You Wish For!

Now, before that back door opens and Claude rejoins the world of his normal domestic life, information about his character and temperament is necessary to fully appreciate the import of this opportunity.

Item #1: the 24-hour mull-over suited him not because he'd have more time to deliberate conscientiously, but, rather, because it took him off the hook for a bit.

Item #2: He disliked making decisions of a meaningful kind. He preferred easily managed choices, such as between Papa John's pizza or steamed broccoli, "Everybody Loves Raymond" or figure skating. He'd gone to the University of North Texas nearby because many friends had, majored in business and rushed Theta Chi for the same reason, worked for his father-in-law's heating and AC business because the old guy said he needed him, married Jacey because she wanted it so much, had Matthew and Becca because they just happened. He considered himself content. So—

Item #3: Unlike many former frat brothers, coworkers, and present pals, he had no burning desire to do something else, be somewhere else, be someone else, or be with someone else. When he and Jacey bought up from their starter home years ago it was mostly because Jacey pushed for it. She usually planned their vacations, visits to their kids in Austin and San Antonio, what dinner parties they attended or hosted, whether they went to church or skipped it.

Having a genie grant him one unexpected, unsolicited wish was the worst thing that had happened in good while. He would have to discover what in his life he most lacked and/or what he most wanted. They might be the same, but, then again. A part of him urged spending it recklessly in a rush just to shake the monkey off his back.

Jacey and Wendy were seated elbows to the kitchen table. Between them was what appeared to be a child's heap o' pirate treasure, and they were poking it with index fingers and shunting pieces out for closer inspection.

"What's that?"

"Costume jewelry." Jacey lifted a clump of burnished metal glittering with colored stones to the light and squinted at it.

"I know that. I mean what's it for?"

The women laughed. "We don't know yet," said Jacey. "We got a grocery sack full for ten dollars."

"We might turn up something fabulous," said Wendy.

"Something old," said Jacey.

"Or just wonderful," said Wendy.

"Will it make your lives any better?"

They women shot him looks of muted surprise mingled with suspicion, as if he were criticizing them. Jacey snickered. "No, but it passes the time in a harmless way," she said pointedly.

"I didn't mean anything," Claude said. "Honest."

"If we don't unearth a prize, we'll give it all away to little girls," said Wendy.

"Poor girls," said Jacey. "Rich girls would just turn up their noses."

A strangled cry issued from elsewhere in the house.

"Would you please see what Daddy wants?"

Claude found Arliss in the family room. His wheelchair had wedged between the recliner and the coffee table probably because he'd tried to push himself up to the TV to change channels rather than use the remote. Hands on the wheels, he was grunting ferociously and banging the chair repeatedly against the table to bulldoze it aside. He was a strong old coot. Years ago, Claude once saw him heave a dozen hundred-pound bags of cement from the ground into a pickup bed without stopping for breath. He still had a broom of thick white hair stiffly upright like a rooster's comb and a long ruddy face grizzled with prickly stubble. His eyesight was perfect but he was deaf as a post, and they'd long since given up equipping him with hearing aids. They'd insert them but as soon as they turned their backs, he'd pop them out and toss them under the furniture or in the trash cans.

"Arliss! Hold on, there! You're caught up." Claude grasped the handles and eased Arliss backward to his usual spot by the archway into the dining room.

"Arrgg got got GOT dd!" Arliss groaned. Claude was pretty good at translating the old fellow's stroke-crippled utterances, and this one was "Aw, goddamnit!"

Claude eased onto the sofa, picked up the remote.

"How about Baylor and TCU?" Claude shouted when he'd surfed up to FoxSports Southwest. Arliss grunted. Claude figured it was the same to Arliss one way or the other, but it seemed right to ask. Third quarter. TCU 17 Baylor 3.

"We got a good contract from a little school district up north of McKinney," Claude declared after a while, though he was fairly certain Arliss didn't hear him. When Arliss stroked out two years ago, Claude became the COO. Since it involved making decisions that effected other peoples' lives, he was a very reluctant boss, and half the time he toted his decisions home to Jacey and let her help him assess the options.

Arliss was entranced by the dance of colored lights on the screen. Might be asleep with his eyes open, like a horse.

"Arliss, if you could have one wish, what would it be?"

Arliss closed his eyes.

"World peace?"

Jacey passed by the archway. "Who're you talking to, the TV?"

"Arliss."

"I don't think he's listening."

"That's not unusual."

She vanished. The network commentators' moronic blather annoyed him, so he hit the mute.

"Oh, I know what you'd want." He turned toward the old man. His head and fallen with his chin to his chest.

By the time Wendy had gone and Jacey had made a salad and warmed up the leftover King Ranch chicken casserole, Claude had drifted into denial, the way you do when a doctor tells you not to worry so you don't, even when you know he's got no crystal ball. He'd dreamed up the vase and the genie Sybil. He'd never considered himself particularly imaginative, though he easily conjured up vivid worst-case scenarios about the health or whereabouts of his loved ones, and he was known to pessimistically overestimate the time and trouble any work order was likely to take. Despite this, he called himself an optimist simply because he felt capable of responding in a forthright way to all imagined catastrophes.

By the time he and Jacey had finished watching "48 Hours Mystery" and Jacey had rolled Arliss off to his bedroom, Claude was wondering why he'd had such a weird fantasy—it was so real, it went beyond a silly daydream. Could such a daydream be provoked by a subterranean rumbling in a person's unrealized thoughts about his life? Was he discontented? What could he wish for? It would be monumentally stupid to waste one granted wish on any gadget you could buy with a credit card, that's for sure. But something less tangible but more essential—your youth, for example! But what about Jacey and the kids—would his wish drag them back to that time and place without their consent? (In which case the kids would be unborn.) Could he be both here and there? How would that work?

Jacey, reading her new Patricia Cornwell.

"How's your book?"

"Good so far."

He let her read a few more paragraphs. "Jacey, if you had one wish, what would it be?"

"To read this book in peace."

"No kidding, I want to know."

"Really?" She turned to him, closed the book's cover over the place-holding hand. "Why do you want to know?"

"I'm curious if there's anything about your life you'd change if you had a chance."

She leaned toward him, slid her glasses down. "What's with you?"

"Nothing. I'm just asking, for God's sake."

"Where'd the question come from?"

He shrugged. "Nowhere, really. Just a thought."

"What would you wish for?"

"I asked first."

She turned back to the novel and pushed her glasses up her nose. She flipped a page. "For one of our kids to go to law school and the other to get married and give us a grandchild."

Claude laughed. "That's it?"

"Yep. Oh, and come back and live nearby when they're all grown up." Here she gazed dreamily at the ceiling. "Just close enough that we could drive there on a Sunday morning and have lunch with them, or they could come here."

"Those things could happen without the help of a supernatural power."

"Well, sure! You didn't ask me to wish for something that couldn't possibly happen! Is that what yours is?"

"No. I don't know yet what mine is. I'll have to think about it."

He closed his eyes as if he would now consider the question, and Jacey, eager to read, allowed him that pretense. It wasn't altogether a pose. He was ruminating on it. It surprised him that Jacey hadn't wished better health for her father, since that apparently wasn't going to happen without such help.

Her wish? A genie could phone that one in. A genie might even be downright insulted to fix something you could do yourself. Jacey could easily convince Matthew to live within a hour's radius of his mother. Becca would be a tougher case, though you wouldn't have to rub magic lamps to get that done.

He woke up at 2 with his stomach growling. He slipped out of bed, poked his head into Arliss's room, then went downstairs to the kitchen. But it turned out nothing seemed appetizing, so he sat at the table quietly belching his way through a diet Coke. He tried to think of something he might like to eat. His mother's apricot fried pies crept to mind. He'd watch her roll the dough out flat like a pie crust then cut it into circles. She stewed dried apricots with sugar and spices, and that filling was then heaped on half a circle. The other half was folded over it, the edges were crimped with the tines of a fork. The pies were then dunked in her deep-fryer like doughnuts, then drained, cooled, and sprinkled with confectioner's sugar. Sweet and tart. He would not have their like again in his lifetime. His mother's apricot fried pies shot to the top of his wish list.

Soon he was trudging down a thorny path to a station of his own cross. His mother had died in a small-town nursing home four hours away where she'd spent the previous year out of her head with Alzheimer's. The place was cheap and plain and grim even while costly, and it so depressed him that Jacey wound up going on his behalf except for three visits, all holidays when the place was packed with other visitors. When she could no longer understand what he said to her or, then, even seem to hear him when he tried to speak, he realized he was left holding a bag full of unspoken words that he'd wanted to say. But hadn't. The last time he'd gone, Jacey said, "Poor thing. She doesn't have any idea who we are or where she is." He said, "Thank God!" His worst thought was that she would open her eyes and ears and be fully cognizant that she was living in a locked-down cinderblock cell with a linoleum floor, sleeping on a bed made about ankle-height to prevent falls, a rubber sheet underneath her and a different orderly every day man-handling her like a truculent doll to wipe her clean and change her diaper.

The night air was a damp wool blanket against his face, bug-thick, sawn to pieces by the ratchety hack of cicadas. He reached inside the door to his workshop and flicked on the overhead light. The vase stood where he'd left it, the strong halogen lamp over the work space flooding it with museum-like drama. He kept telling himself he was being stupid—there's no genie!!! He ought to go back to bed or read until he got sleepy. Coming out here to test the vase made him feel like a superstitious ninny. He was an educated man capable of installing software on the office PCs, for God's sake. He didn't believe nine-tenths of the supposedly miraculous crap that he'd heard about in sermons over the past five decades.

Yet, here he was.

He drew a deep breath. His fingers trembled and left the slightest sheen of dew from their pads on the cool green surface.

"Hello, you've reached Genies Universal, Incorporated! How can I help you?"

He opened his mouth but nothing came, he was that surprised by a live voice. He bent and peeked into the vase.

"Hello?"

"Hello, sir! If you would be so kind to state your wish, please?"

The woman had an Indian accent, like the customer service reps of his bank. Bangalore, he guessed.

"Uh, could I speak to Sybil, please?"

"Yes, I am Sybil, sir!"

"You are? Well, I spoke to another one earlier today."

"Oh, sir, she is gone for the evening. But I will be pleased to assist you! I must let you know that this call might be monitored for quality assurance purposes."

He supposed he should've called during regular business hours, but who would know a genie's regular hours?

"Well, she told me I could have twenty-four hours for my wish, but I wondered if I could discuss it with somebody before I step into the deal with both feet."

"Step into the ideal with bow feet, sir?"

"You know, declare my wish for sure."

"Excuse me, sir, but would you mind holding while I check the records?"

That banjo and minstrels tune swelled up suddenly as this Sybil cut off her headset. Where'd they get this music? It was like the soundtrack to a 30s musical about the wonderful Old South. Uncle Remus music. He felt silly standing at his workbench with his palms cupped about the hips of the vase as if he and it were about to mambo—did "hold" mean literally?

"Hello, sir! Thank you for your patience. My supervisor has confirmed that you indeed have not received your wish yet."

"Yes, I know. My question was could I talk to somebody about it first?"

"Certainly, sir! Feel free to do so."

"Oh, great! Well, then, here's what I was thinking–"

"Oh, sir! I am most sorry. We cannot discuss it, but you are surely free to talk to anyone in your circle of acquaintanceship, confidence, or influence."

He wasn't about to utter word one to any living soul about this. "Okay, look. Here's what I want. I want to tell my mother some things I didn't say before she died."

A silence at the other end unnerved him. "Are you there?"

"Oh, yes sir! Sorry! I am getting ready the necessary paperwork."

"So that's... possible?"

"Oh, yes, sir. Very common, sir."

He was both relieved and deflated to hear that the wish he'd so agonized over was like choosing vanilla for your cone.

He'd swear he heard the click of computer keys.

"Sir, I must need ask you a few questions?"

"Okay."

"Will this be a one-time meeting or a continuing relationship?"

"I... I haven't thought about it. One time, I suppose." Now why did he choose that? "I mean, will she be, uh, coming back to life?"

"In a manner of speaking, sir. At what point along the continuum of time should we shed-yule your rendezvous?"

"Uh, make it some time when...Senior prom night! Yeah. She thought I was handsome in my tux. She made me bring Jacey back to the house so she could take our picture, and she told me she was so, so proud of me. There were tears in her eyes. I wanted to say..." He blushed furiously. None of Sybil-from-Bangalore's bee's-wax, by God!

More tapping of keys. A whirring sound. Suddenly, a cylinder of rolled papers jutted out of the mouth. He pulled it free.

"What's this?"

"Our standard contract, sir. It's basically a waiver indemnifying us against damages occurring due to unforeseen or unintended consequences."

He pressed it flat on the workbench. Five pages, 2-pt font, single-spaced. Last paragraph dropped precipitously off to a horizontal line for his signature. It'd take a week to read this. It was like the legal boilerplate he was required to agree to when installing software or paying bills online - Nobody really read this stuff, right?

"What kind of consequences?"

"Oh, sir–unintended and unforeseen ones, as I said."

"Can you give me an example?"

"Oh, sir, I'm afraid they would not be unforeseen in such a case."

He fell momentarily into a ruminant funk. The summer he was 16, he and a buddy secretly ran away to join a crew in the panhandle harvesting wheat and didn't let his folks know where he was for ten days out of fear they'd lasso him back. "You about worried your mother sick to death," his dad said later after he finally broke down, broke, and called from Kansas. "Then when she heard you weren't dead in a ditch but were just being thoughtless and cruel, it about broke her heart." He never apologized; instead, he argued that he was old enough to make his own spending money and they should be proud he was being a man instead of carrying on so about his going off.

What possible harm could come from standing before her now and saying, "Momma, I'm really sorry. I know you must've been, well, sick with worry."

Or the time that he and Jacey didn't invite her and his dad to Matthew's first birthday party because their college friends would be there, some of whom would likely wind up in the back yard toking on a doobie, and Claude planned to lay out good hootch and have cigars and a boom box blasting the Eagles or Charlie Daniels or Asleep at the Wheel and he didn't want to endure even her tacit disapproval. At the time, she and his dad dressed like farm people from the 50s, his dad in Dickies jeans and corny Western shirts with snap buttons, and his mom in tired old cotton dresses with faded floral patterns and black shoes that looked orthopedic even if they weren't. Of course, they dropped by that night to bring Matthew a present—the first birthday of their first grandchild—not even knowing a party was in progress, and when his dad had pulled his old International to the curb and it became obvious to them, his mother stayed in the truck and his dad brought the present to the door. Claude was in the back yard, and Jacey saw his dad coming up the walk and sent a friend to answer the knock. Claude heard about it later. His mother never mentioned it, and he never apologized, thinking that if she didn't mention it and he didn't either, then no harm had been done.

What possible harm could come from standing before her now and saying, "Momma, I'm really sorry. I know you must've been, well, very hurt."

And it wasn't just apologies in that bag of orphaned words. Thank you for sending me off every day of grammar school with a lunch box full of stuff you knew I loved—deviled ham and roast beef sandwiches, hand-crafted sugar and oatmeal cookies. Thank you for sitting me on your lap and teaching me to read. Thank you for telling me that you were happy that I'd chosen Jacey as my bride. Etcetcetcetcetera.

Claude imagined his mother standing—sitting?—in front of him at some point in their lives prior to her Alzheimer's listening to his confession. Thanking him. Bawling with joy, most likely. She ought to, anyway.

And then. And then? Sorry, Mom, but you've got to lie back down in your grave now. Or she stays alive from that moment on to endure once again the harrowing descent into bad health and dementia and a miserable fucking end? All to hear his belated valentine?

"Hey!" He blew into the vase. "Hello?" The system seemed to have disconnected while he gnawed so ferociously on his worry bone, so he had to rub the thing and fret through the voice-mail cycle and hold until he reached a live genie who said, in a male voice, "Hello, I am Sybil! What is your wish?"

Claude thrust a baleful eye into the vase. Sure enough, a young fellow with dark hair, glasses magnifying his brown, thick-lashed eyes. Claude explained about his two other Sybils and how he'd been considering a wish and that when he'd asked the second Sybil if his mother would actually be brought back to life "she told me and I quote 'in a manner of speaking.' Would you mind clarifying that?"

"It would be a holographic image of her, Sir."

"Not my real mother, then."

"Sir, we cannot raise the dead. I'm sorry, sir, if someone gave you that impression."

"What possible good is it to spill my guts to a holograph?"

"Sir, this is not for us to say. But it might ease your spirits, perhaps?" this fellow Sybil offered uncertainly.

"Hardly."

"Perhaps you'd like to choose a consolation wish, then? Money is a very popular option." The genie chuckled. "Money is no object, Sir."

If they'd been conversing on a telephone, Claude would've slammed down the receiver. But he didn't know how to hang up on a genie with such a flourish.

"Thanks for nothing!" Claude growled. "I'll get back to you."

When he was sure the genie had vanished forthwith probably for his tiffin, Claude reached above the workbench and plucked his steel-handled claw hammer with a rubber grip off a peg. He raised the hammer above the vase. He aimed and cocked, breathed in and out. We could ply the tricks of our trade and intercut between the quivering upraised hammer, Claude's furious grimace, the shimmering green vase, milk the suspense to the last drop (vase-hammerface, vasehammerface, etc.), but such cheap gimmicks would amount to little once we remember who he is—a person who dislikes making choices, especially those that he can't call back.

He lowered the hammer and stared at the vase for a long while.

He rummaged about and found a cardboard box, filled the box with foam pellets, laid the vase in it, sealed the box with tape.

It was now about 3:30 a.m. He drove his Silverado several blocks to the all-night Albertson's, where he bought silver foil wrapping paper and a bright red bow, a box of buckwheat pancake batter, a carton of fresh blueberries, and a large bouquet of assorted flowers, at least two of which Claude knew to be lilies.

When Jacey came down from the bedroom, a little curious and alarmed as to why he'd apparently left their bed and was now in the kitchen cooking at dawn, he said, "Sit down, honey. The coffee's ready."

"Flowers," she murmured groggily.

"That's right. And buckwheat cakes with blueberries just like you like them."

"How come?"

"Because you're my very precious treasure."

"Huh," she said.

"I need for you to know that I know that. Did you hear it?"

She smiled. "You're nuts."

Claude left for work. On his way to the office, he called her on his cell and told her to go find the gift he'd left her on his workbench.

Big Rig

The storekeeper's daughter wore her glossy black hair in one braid long as her arm. The boy, Robert, had never seen that—girls wore pony-tails, but this hairdo looked exotic. He'd been rooting in the gear box of the big diesel truck to retrieve two suitcases and an old gym bag. He happened to look up when the girl—about his age, he hoped—strode from the back of the store and took the bald sandy path between the mesquites to an outhouse. She was carrying a toilet paper roll with her thumb in the tube. The braid pendulumed where her jeans neatly snugged her hips. She'd tucked a red t-shirt into the beltless waistband. That she was carrying toilet paper to the outhouse made his face flush as his imagination leapfrogged his conscience.

His boss and the other helper had been here before. On the way, Mr. Clyde called the storekeeper's daughter that Messkin gal with a sweet ass. He razzed Leroy about how the girl had shot him down when Leroy had tried to sweet-talk her. Leroy scoffed—he wouldn't touch her with Clyde's ten-foot pole. Mr. Clyde laughed—he was flattered that Leroy thought he had one. Robert wasn't used to hearing men josh this way; though embarrassed, he noted how this banter went so he might master it or at least participate skillfully enough to be invisible in the pack.

Judging from the dorsal view, this was she. The boy lived in such an opaque cocoon of the 1950s that his notions about girls, so-called Mexican or otherwise, were contradictory, even preposterous. Older males talked about going to "Boy's Town" in Nuevo Laredo, Ciudad Acuña, or Juarez, where apparently being a whore was winked at by the law. The legendary potion Spanish fly, the little cartoon books depicting Dagwood and Blondie doing it with outsized organs—these too were procured in Mexican border towns. He and the two men had travelled far enough on this day to be only a couple hours north of the Rio Grande.

The only "Mexican" girl he knew personally had been in his typing class; Pauline Torres wore thick glasses and long dresses and belonged to the Latin and Journalism clubs. Around her neck hung a cross (not a crucifix) on a fine gold chain. Cool, quiet, cautious, Pauline was the opposite of hot-blooded, passionate women who clacked castanets as they stomped about, seemingly so dangerous and angry. Most Mexican-American girls in his town a couple hundred miles to the north attended Catholic school, where during recess they milled about in white blouses and dark blue skirts as if in an army.

The girl stepped inside the outhouse, left the door wide open, set down the roll, then pirouetted on her heels and headed back up the path. Robert ducked behind the cab of the truck. Even from this distance her face was like a new quarter you unexpectedly spot on the ground.

The sun had disappeared over the roof, and the girl vanished in a shadow near the door, backlit briefly as a silhouette. The sky to the east had a pale violent tinge as twilight seeped toward him, and a bull bat dove invisibly past his head with a flutter. The air was cooling fast. Nearby, a clutch of cattle trudged toward home, white faces glowing like ghost masks. The three-man crew had driven deep into the arroyo-slashed emptiness of the Trans-Pecos, a land of long vistas, red-flanked mesas, boulders big as refrigerators, and hardly a living being to be seen other than antelope galloping in the distance, rabbits, and buzzards scouting breakfast hidden in thickets.

Out of nowhere they'd pulled up to the Garcia General Store sitting alone as if dropped by a tornado where two remote country highways crossed. So far as Robert could tell, the closest house or business lay miles away, though behind the store were sheds and a corral. Like from an old Western, the two-story wooden building had a covered porch. On it stood two metal lawn chairs, and Robert's hip knocked the green one over as he wrestled the valises through the screen door. When he shouldered the tin Wonder Bread banner affixed to the inner door, bells jingled inside.

Mr. Clyde and Leroy stood at a counter where a salty-haired Mexican fellow was tallying up their purchases on an old crank register with metal tabs that popped up in a window. Loaf of white bread, cans of Vienna sausage and pork and beans, and sticks of jerky, though the dark stringy twigs weren't wrapped. The labels weren't Van Camp. On his first excursion overnight as an employee with co-workers, eating off-brand beans and homemade jerky presented another challenge. The stringed jerky hung from a wall hook below a sign hand-lettered "deer sausage." Presently a cluster of flies fed on it, so he wouldn't eat it no matter how much ribbing he'd take.

While Mr. Clyde settled their bill, Robert strolled the aisles presumably inspecting the inventory (motor oil, Spam, brass screws, horse bridles, Ivory soap, double-bladed axe) but kept a sidelong surveillance on the open doorway to the rear. Strands of colored glass beads draped from the header, bringing to mind crystal balls, tents, and silk scarves. The girl probably lived back there. Maybe she'd part the beaded curtain like coming up from a dive, and he'd get a closer look.

Mr. Clyde trooped them up an outside staircase to a big room on the second story. One battered chest with six drawers, three old Army surplus cots perpendicular to the three windows, three along the inner wall. The boy hung back at the door gripping the gym bag, waiting, as if choosing a urinal. Mr. Clyde took a cot at the room's far end under a window, and Leroy took another, leaving an empty between them; Robert then chose one against the wall. The two men tossed their suitcases onto their cots, then Mr. Clyde set the food on the middle bunk as if on a table.

"C.B., go get them drinks," Mr. Clyde said to him.

"Yes sir," said Robert.

"And don't be dawdlin," said Leroy.

Leroy was ten years older but only a helper, too. It always felt good to ignore his wisecracks and unauthorized orders. Enduring Mr. Clyde's nickname was humiliating enough.

The girl was watering galvanized tubs of red geraniums with a can that had a big blossom head such as Alice used in his childhood illustrated edition. He peered at the landscape, now drenched in ethereal lavender light. He pretended to appreciate the view. She ignored his presence.

Finally, he said, "Uh, hello."

She smiled, waggled the sprinkler head as if to reply. She murmured either "hello" or "hola." She had huge brown eyes fit for drowning in. Long black lashes. Gazing into her face made him swallow.

He poked his chest with his thumb. "Robert. Friends, amigos, say Bobby."

"Roberto," she said with a tiny smile.

"What is your name?" He placed each word slowly on the air.

"My name is Victoria." She also gave each word its own space. Her "i"s were long "e"s—ees Veektoreea—and he reeled a bit inside. His hands went sweaty.

He stifled his trembling and pointed to the huge diesel truck parked along the road. Very slowly and patiently, using a simple vocabulary, he told her about their work. A large section of a drilling rig's derrick lay horizontally with the big end chained to the truck bed, and the derrick's top was fixed to a trailer of big-tired wheels fifty feet behind it. They called the top part a "crow's nest," he told her, like on the mast of old sailing ships. This truck and the pickup

103

with the CAUTION OVERSIZE LOAD banner were part of a caravan taking parts of the rig from where it had finished drilling to a new pad where they would meet to reassemble it.

Thus the text of his story. The subtext: he felt immensely proud of this manly work. It was his first job no boy could do. He stood with his feet wide apart and his arms crossed over his chest to show off his new biceps. No more tossing papers from his bike, sacking in the supermarket, mowing lawns. His father was a veep with an oil company that gave the trucking firm a lot of business. Robert was eager to show his father and himself that he was up to lifting, heaving, and sweating through a blistering day of hard labor. So far, he'd done well, as Mr. Clyde often plucked him from the pool of helpers—they called them "swampers"—gaggled in the company's yard each morning. It hadn't dawned on him until a moment ago, though, that his Working With Big Machines might impress girls. As he patiently unreeled his tale, he wondered if she understood. She'd look up from watering and smile briefly. He recalled his manners.

"Do you go to school?"

"School?"

"Yes. Uh—" He searched for the word. "Escuela?"

"Oh!" She laughed. She straightened to face him squarely. "Yes, the bus picks me up right here and takes me into McCamey. Except during football season because I have cheerleader practice and my mother has to get me there earlier."

Roberto blushed.

"And sometimes after school I have to stay because we have a meeting of the National Honor Society or Future Farmers or something."

She had laid it the English on thick to mock his presumption, but he had to stand and take it. He kept nodding agreeably. He yearned to back up time, just go out to the truck without having spoken. He would miss this humiliation and she'd still be full of intriguing mystery and the possibility of misadventure. Maybe, he supposed, her smart-aleck streak rose from that hot blood finding an outlet. He feared she'd turn that on him full force.

"I'm in the NHS at my high school," was the best he could do. "I'll be a junior."

"Senior."

Another spike to his heart. Probably a quarterback all riled to hear that "Roberto" (a joke, right?) had flirted and that his thoughts were, uh, ungentlemanly. Chastened, he decided the manly thing was courtesy.

"Well, nice to meet you. I gotta go get the beer cooler." He dipped his head toward the truck.

"Mucho gusto," she said to his back with a lilt that suggested an inward giggle.

Was her Spanish meant to rib or compliment him? He hoped the implication that the beer was for him seeped into her presumptions. Not a virgin, but a novice: he and pals had pilfered a big brother's stash on prior occasions, but he didn't expect to be offered one from this cooler.

The cooler was a big metal box encasing 24 cans of Lone Star and the two Dr. Peppers he'd bought for himself; at a meat locker in Big Spring they'd bought big chunks of clear ice meant to last them through tomorrow. Carrying the chest would normally require two men, but he believed that wrangling it alone was part of his initiation. He tugged it off the truck bed and onto one shoulder, staggered up the stoop to the porch—the girl had gone, unfortunately, as she could've witnessed his feat—and up the long outside staircase.

"About fucking time. You been having a little party with Rosy Palm?"

Mr. Clyde said, "Old Pelvis here's getting thirsty. He ate more than his share."

To Mr. Clyde, the boy said, "They wanted to know where we'd brought the rig from."

They'd left him an opened can of Vienna sausage and a half can of pork and beans, two sticks of jerky, several slices of bread. No utensils. Having to dig into the grub with his filthy fingers like a hobo made him cringe.

"I gotta piss."

At the end of the hall, the door to the upper story's bathroom stood ajar. Except in a campground, he'd never seen such primitive fixtures: a big tin funnel nailed to a stud tubed through the wall and presumably down outside, but to crap you'd use the outhouse. Aside from that, only a basin streaked with rust under a single tap. He pissed to make his lie right to himself, but no soap was there to wash with. He feared his pimples had grown to ruddy hillocks on his brow, but the wall over the basin showed two big screw holes and an unpainted square where maybe a medicine cabinet once hung. A small consolation—this would be harder on Leroy, who combed his long black greasy hair incessantly to emulate The King. Since Elvis's trademark style included that single curl across his brow, Leroy kept very busy tinkering so that one long lock dangled just so; he was often the last to leave the truck when they stopped for coffee or lunch because waitresses would need to be made aware of the resemblance, which, to Robert, was only faint at best. Leroy acted out the role—cocky, smirky, all baritone baloney with a phony Dixie accent. It gratified Robert that some clearly thought Leroy was a buffoon. But—this perplexed him no end—others fell for it. That they reacted made it worth considering.

After he'd scrubbed his hands by holding them under the cold water, he swiped them on his dirty jeans.

Mr. Clyde and Leroy were deep into their second or third beers. Ford or Chevy? An endless debate. Last year Leroy bought a two-year-old '57 Chevy with the big V-8, hardtop, blue over white. Mr. Clyde had told Robert he guessed Leroy's check got et up by payments, that part left from child support. To Robert, the car was a dazzling automotive wonder, the only thing in Leroy's life he envied. He admired the engineering but also the social utility; common lore said girls (women) chose a man by what car he drove. Robert's primary ambition wasn't to be a doctor, lawyer, test pilot, or forest ranger—it was to make enough this summer to meet his dad's 50/50 challenge. Come fall, a car he called his own would be parked in the student lot. Nothing so fine as that '57 Chevy (Leroy called it his cock wagon), but driving his own wheels to school would instantly elevate him: you could give a girl a ride; on a date, you weren't in your parents' old-fart sedan, so you needn't worry about spills (beer, bodily fluids) or what might be hoarded under the seat (rubbers, cigarettes).

While Leroy regaled Mr. Clyde with a yarn about a drag-racing triumph that Robert had already heard, Robert finished off their leavings. He plucked the Vienna sausages from the can with his fingers and put them between two slices of bread, wolfed that down, then drank the juice and the pork and beans from the open can. He steeled himself to bite into the jerky but found it tasty, with a peppery tang, satisfying to chew. He pictured Victoria at supper with her parents—what'd they have? If he was her boyfriend, he'd be eager to be invited; he wasn't a bit afraid of Mexican food.

He stood and dug in the cooler for a Dr. Pepper. Mr Clyde said, "C.B., you want one of them beers, hep yourself."

"He ain't old enough and you know it."

"When did you have your first brew?"

Leroy snorted. "Thirteen. My old man caught me sneaking it out of the ice box. He made me drink a whole six-pack right in front of him."

"I bet you got dog sick," said Robert.

"Hell yes! Didn't keep me from guzzling a bunch more, though."

Robert peered into the cooler to stall. He had to trust nobody would tell his parents. He drew out a cold can. Mr. Clyde gestured for it, so he passed it. Mr. Clyde punctured the top, gave it back. While they watched, he took a swig.

'Aw hellfire, Bobby, you can do better than that."

"I ain't used to it so cold," he said to Leroy. His father didn't know he quaffed an occasional beer, and his mother didn't know he ever said ain't. He took a braver slug and gulped. Bitter taste.

He sipped the beer while Mr. Clyde and Leroy between them put away a dozen. Mr. Clyde reminisced about his days in Korea and Japan with the Air Force, and Leroy tried to match him with graphic snippets of his love life now that he and his old lady had split the blanket. That led to a long bitter monologue about his ex-wife, Jeanie. Robert and Mr. Clyde had heard it all before. Ball-buster, big spender, always running around with her pals, all of them sluts and lounge lizards, and the way she always told it they went in a flock together to the honky-tonks so they could dance or not when they were asked but not be pestered by peckerwoods, and after last call they'd pile back into the car they'd all come in—all a bunch of fucking lies!

Leroy's ex-wife was a checker at the supermarket where Robert's family shopped. She was always friendly with his mother. Behind the register, wearing the green apron, tendrils of blonde hair escaping the rubber-band noose above her nape and smudges of weariness under her green eyes, it was hard to imagine a wanton temptress flinging herself at fellows. She and Leroy married soon as they graduated high school but divorced last year. A few months ago, Leroy had been charged with assaulting a man whom he'd spied driving around with Jeanie. He'd been following her every night, parking outside his old house and driving off only when she'd step onto the porch and mime calling the police to enforce a court order.

Though Leroy didn't talk about their four-year-old daughter, Robert had seen that the picture slots in his wallet held snaps only of her.

Robert believed he'd be too proud to stalk a girl who rejected him. He wouldn't let her know she'd wounded him, by God. Besides, that only happened to people like Leroy. His parents had been together since time began, and he'd not heard of anyone in his family divorcing.

Robert drifted away. He could go down to the porch on the chance that she'd show up. Just enjoying the evening, though that sounded like a corny movie. Or they sent me to the truck for cigars. He could smoke one, maybe. They don't like the stink, wanted me to come down here to smoke it. She sidles up to a porch pillar and entwines herself around it, peekaboos him. Do you ever get lonely way out here? Jes, sometime eet ees lonely.

Maybe a walk through the pastures, moon enough for it. Hold her hand. Then his arm around her small waist, hip to hip. One time on a church hay ride, he and Gabby—

"Hey, C.B., get over here—we need a third." Mr. Clyde was shuffling cards.

"You know how to play stud poker?" asked Leroy.

Robert nodded. The version someone at church camp taught him was called "Dr. Pepper Poker" because 10s, 2s, and 4s, were wild, along with one-eyed Jacks.

To Mr. Clyde he said, "I haven't played in a while. I'm not sure I remember what beats what."

Leroy cackled. "We'll teach you as we go along."

He sat on the cooler at the end of the unused cot between the men. Mr. Clyde dealt them down and up cards. Robert was surprised to learn that they'd play with their real money and not with matchsticks. Mr. Clyde sketched out how the hands went one pair, two, three of a kind, straight, flush, full house, four of a kind, straight flush.

Robert made mistakes that were obvious soon after he'd made them, such as not paying close attention to the up cards and not thinking of how many of each were available in a deck. In an hour he'd lost all his money. It was meant to buy two more meals they'd eat tomorrow. He lost it equally to both men. Neither excused his greenness; neither offered his money back.

Leroy said, "You wanna borrow a couple bucks?"
He predicted he'd lose those too and be in hock to Leroy. "Naw, thanks."

Leroy and Mr. Clyde shifted to black jack, trading off as dealer and player. The buzz from that first beer had worn off, and, as if to console himself or prove that losing at poker didn't diminish his incipient manhood, he got another. He drank and watched them for a bit, but being the sidelined loser felt humiliating, so he slipped off without comment onto the landing.

Mr. Clyde had betrayed him somehow. He'd have to go without breakfast and lunch tomorrow or beg Mr. Clyde for a loan or a draw against his pay. He'd presumed that a boss was a fatherly supervisor who'd look out for his welfare. Had Mr. Clyde and Leroy schemed to milk him of his cash? Maybe they were jealous his family was "comfortable" (his parents' word), a jealousy reflected in Mr. Clyde's calling him "C.B." When first asked what grade he was in, Robert had replied the way his father would've answered on

108

his behalf: "I'll be a junior. I'm on the college bound track." It only meant that you took advanced courses in English, math, and social studies, along with foreign languages. But Mr. Clyde had chuckled. "College bound, huh? Well, C.B., I went to Hard Knocks U, myself." He shook off these sorry thoughts. After all, they'd treated him like a man, right? A man buys into a poker game at his own risk, and if he loses, tough shit. The loss is the price of poker lessons.

A long low shed lay some yards behind the store with a corral attached. Light flickered through cracks in the siding, as if from a carried lantern. Horse stalls, maybe. Cow shed. She'd mentioned the FFA—was she feeding and watering livestock? Farmer's daughter!

The moon had risen, and from his high perch, leaning on the rail, the pale white light overlay the gently rolling scrubland. The heavens were a milky wash of stars beyond the moon, and he thought how nice to be lying on a blanket with a girl and peering at that sky. Not just Victoria. Guys talked about "types" they liked: blondes and redheads, mostly, usually with big tits. He'd not discovered his special type. So far, he liked skinny girls and chubby girls freckled or not with brown, blonde, red, or black hair and with blue, brown, and green eyes, tall and short. He liked girls who rode bicycles and read books and girls who were cheerleaders and girls who played softball, girls who rode horses and those who could whistle and those who liked to dance or play the viola. He liked smart girls, even those who didn't hide it; he liked girls who talked a lot and girls who were silent and mysterious. He liked to hear girls sing any song, and he liked the fine hair on their forearms and napes. He liked the way they smelled when they weren't wearing perfume and when they were. As for breasts, there was no wrong size.

Since the fifth grade, he'd had at least a dozen girlfriends, though not all knew they were, and, though he'd kissed most and often been kissed back, he'd only once scored a feel below the waist, Patsy Baxter's inner thigh, very near a cotton-clad spot so heated he felt the radiation on the back of his hand. Though it was fleeting, the memory had rooted very deep.

Would Victoria show up again? He replayed their encounter on the porch. He revised dialogue. As a senior and fellow NHS member, she'd probably appreciate hearing he took the college bound courses—maybe she was on a similar track. What college are you applying to? What are your hobbies? Do you go to the movies around here? A drive-in? What kind of music do you like? Elvis? Pat Boone? The Platters?

He guessed that was how you kept a conversation up. He never felt too shy with girls, just uncertain because he wasn't sure what worked.

The light in the shed blinked, went out. He waited awhile but nothing more happened.

Mr. Clyde was undressing in his corner, back to the room. He wore baggy boxer shorts decorated with hound dogs; the elastic was spent so the shorts drooped below his butt crack—this was a perplexing and embarrassing revelation, though Robert had no idea why. Mr. Clyde was a widower who lived alone, his grown children and grandchildren somewhere far.

Beer cans stood on the window sills or lay on the floor. Robert counted seventeen. Mr. Clyde took a few steps backward and collapsed with grunt onto the cot. He belched, sighed, groaned, fought kicking to get under the top sheet and one thin blanket that made up their linens. He had folded up his clothing as a pillow. He yawned, smacked his lips. His grey hair was all a tangle. He drew the blanket up over his shoulder.

Leroy sat glaring out the window, elbow on a knee and his chin propped by his palm. Either he didn't hear Robert or chose to ignore him. The toe of his left boot beat a slow cadence on the floor. Robert studied Leroy's humped back. A word came—brooding. Should he say good night? Just in front of Leroy on the sill stood an open can, maybe empty. If Robert were to ask, "You still drinkin'?" and Leroy were to reply, "What's it to you?" he couldn't answer with the truth: Well, if you're still drinking, I don't want to turn my back to you and go to sleep.

Following Mr. Clyde's example, he didn't wash his face or brush his teeth. He quickly slipped off his work shirt and dug out a T-shirt from the gym bag He unlaced his steel-toed work boots and, still in his jeans and socks, lay with his back to the men and pulled the blanket over his head.

He drifted off. Hardly an hour later, the beer woke him and he had to pad groggy and wobbly down the hall in his sock feet to piss. Coming back into their bunk room, he noticed now that Leroy was gone.

Soon as he'd flopped on his cot, a voice or voices came, raised but faint, from outside. He caught his breath, drew up his hearing like tautening a knot, waited. Curiosity and dread clamped him between wanting to ignore his suspicions and needing to face his fear that Leroy was making trouble.

Then it came again. Maybe Mr. Clyde would wake up and take care of this. Or maybe Robert should shake him out of his drunken sleep and tell him Leroy was about to embarrass them and their company.

Like a tattler. It might be that way to Mr. Clyde, and it was possible Mr. Clyde wouldn't care, and Robert would seem a childish alarmist.

When he heard Leroy's angry voice again, he cursed. He pulled his work boots on, half-laced them, went onto the landing. Light gleamed through the siding cracks, so he knew the sounds came from the shed.

She sure shot you down, Pelvis.

I wouldn't touch her with your ten-foot pole.

Leroy must have it in for her. God, why did Robert have to hear this? He could pretend this wasn't his business, right? But Leroy was clearly very drunk, so he could hurt her out of spite.

Robert crept down the stairs, still listening, and when he stepped to the ground, he detected faint yowls, sobs maybe; his nape prickled, his heart thudded against his ribs, and he pictured Leroy grappling Victoria, hand pressed to her mouth, throwing her to the dirt.

He trudged toward the shed feeling he ought to run but couldn't move faster; the half-tied laces whipped about his ankles and caught under his heels. Maybe he was mistaken—could be the storekeeper carrying on, and Robert might blunder into a family squabble. Leroy might be in the pickup snoring away or listening to the radio.

Then like a human tornado siren rose a long slurred cry or sob chopped short by a curse.

Robert sucked up a breath and strode into the shed, confronted a horse nickering and stamping in a stall not six feet from his face. He swung toward the light at the end of the building. Leroy slumped with his back to the wall and Victoria stood nearby with her arms crossed over her breasts.

She was clearly safe, so Robert was free to swagger toward them, fists clenched, brow furrowed as if ready to rescue her.

"He try anything with you?" He glared at Leroy, who buried his face in his hands.

Victoria snorted. "I came out to see what was bothering Pedrito. I found him right there." Her mouth had a sour twist. "Your problem now."

Robert watched her stroll away, her braid swaying across her waist. "Don't let him smoke in here!" she called over her back. Leroy fell onto his side, curled into a ball.

"Jeaannnnieee," he moaned. To stifle his sobs, he ground a fist against his clenched teeth so hard Robert feared they'd score his lips. Leroy was his problem? Leroy's crying made him cringe. He stood by helplessly as Leroy shrugged himself half upright on one elbow and gasped to catch his breath. Leroy's glance flit upward and snagged him.

"GoddamnidBobby." Then a clump of accordioned words that sounded to Robert's ear like I never loved nobody else I swear to God.

"I believe you." Robert ached to slip off free, but his reaction calmed Leroy. He sniffled and swabbed his eyes with the sleeve of his t-shirt. Robert looked toward the horse stall; Victoria had vanished.

"Let's hit the sack, Leroy."

Leroy nodded, but when he stiff-armed himself against the dirt, he couldn't jockey his feet underneath him. Robert grabbed him under his free arm and hoisted him. He slung Leroy's arm across his shoulder; together, like drunken contestants in a sack race, they staggered out of the shed and to the stairs. Leroy stunk of a hard day's work and rank beer sweat. Robert had to heave Leroy up one stair at a time. Halfway, Leroy groaned and his trunk convulsed, so Robert shrugged free quick as he could and propped Leroy against the rail while he puked over the side like a seasick sailor.

Finished, he seemed more sober and levered himself upright by pushing at the banister. He shook his head.

"Goddamnit, Bobby," he moaned. Robert had never seen such an expression of utter sorrow on any man's face, let alone Leroy's. "Bobby, Jeannie ... just ... broke ... my ... fucking ... heart!" He leaned on the rail, burrowed his face into the crook of his elbow, and his shoulders shook.

Feeling helpless, Robert raised a hand to pat Leroy on his back but checked himself. He felt sorry for Leroy, but his compassion was overlaid with contempt: he was dead sure he'd never be in Leroy's pathetic condition.

Leroy was still for a long moment. Robert cleared his throat. "You wanna go on up?"

Leroy raised himself, shook his head like a dog shuddering off water.

"I got her now. Thanks, Bobby."

Mr. Clyde was snoring with huge roaring blasts that made his cheeks billow and his lips flap like a cartoon character. Leroy grinned, put his finger to his lips, and pointed at their boss. Robert managed to smile back. Leroy's sorrow storm had apparently passed. Robert suspected that tomorrow Leroy wouldn't remember it, or he'd pretend it hadn't happened.

Leroy staggered to his bunk, sank onto it with a sigh, then keeled over sideways. In the movies you take the drunk's shoes off and maybe his pants, then cover him, but he'd done enough getting Leroy up here. Lying on his back with his feet on the floor, Leroy fell instantly asleep.

Back on his own cot, Robert lay with his blood pounding his veins, and adrenaline was a piercing needle to his nerves. He listened to their raucous snoring. He yearned to be home in his own bed. He was hungry, tired, thirsty too, and tomorrow's work would take all his effort while the sun beat down all day. Leroy's sobbing his ex-wife's name prodded Robert's memory. It was if Leroy were having a seizure, a seizure of grief and regret and loss. He didn't even seem aware of Victoria.

Robert woke first and looked at his watch—6:10. Late. He rose and dressed, carried the chest out onto the landing and emptied the melted ice water, brought it back and added the few remaining cans of Lone Star and the Dr. Peppers. The racket woke up the two men, and they came around slowly, groaning.

Robert toted the chest out to the truck, and when he walked back to the building, Victoria was sweeping the porch. She was wearing a big blue sweatshirt with an Eagle on the front.

"There's breakfast stuff inside."

"Thanks." He paused at the door. She stopped sweeping, swung the broom around to prod at something on the decking with the butt of the handle. He wanted to apologize for Leroy but couldn't make himself bring it up.

As if reading his mind, she said, "Boy, was your buddy borracho."

"He's not my buddy. I'm sorry that he upset you and your horse."

She shrugged. She stopped sweeping and leaned on the broom handle. "It's okay. It's just that Pedrito's real high-strung." She smiled, right at him, and from it he believed she liked him, that she approved of him, that if he ever came back, they might take that starlit walk.

She went back to sweeping. When it appeared she had no more to say, he went through the door. Victoria's mother had perked coffee, and Mr. Clyde and Leroy were filling their tin cups to take onto the porch. She had also brought out skillet-warmed flour tortillas, and Robert gobbled down two in a row drizzled with honey. He lifted the plate of tortillas to carry out to the men now on the porch, but then he set it down and stood at the counter polishing off their share. Through the front window he watched as Mr. Clyde clamped his temples between middle finger and thumb and winced. Leroy went to the outhouse.

When he and Mr. Clyde walked out to the truck, Mr. Clyde said, "You drive."

Robert almost blurted an objection—he had no license for trucks and absolutely no experience with them. On the other hand, he felt an enormous YES! swamp his whole body like a heat wave.

113

He climbed the three aluminum steps into the high cab and the driver's seat where he sat at the big wheel looking at an array of gauges on the dashboard he'd never known the use of. At his right knee was a gear box with no fewer than three separate shifting levers. When you looked through the windshield, you stood tall over the highway. Victoria was no longer on the porch; he craned his head to see if maybe she was standing at the door, but it was closed. Mr. Clyde had climbed onto the truck bed, and after a moment the passenger door opened, and he levered himself into the seat holding an open can of beer. When Robert couldn't hide his astonishment, Mr. Clyde waved the can at him.

"Hair of the dog." He took a mouthful but screwed up his face as if he'd drunk castor oil. "I'm gonna tell you how to get it moving down the road then don't ask me jack shit until you have to stop, you hear? I need a nap."

"Yes sir."

They started the engine, and because it was a diesel it had to warm up. While it did, Mr. Clyde gave him a five-minute primer in using the gears then told him many other things so fast and in such a jumble they washed over him. Parked ahead, Leroy was at the wheel of the pickup, his driver's window open, cigarette smoke wafting from the cab.

Then they were off. When they segued through the gears and up to 50, Robert checked the big rearview mirror posted on the side of the cab. The huge long derrick trailed behind them—this was like driving the locomotive of a train. The road was empty and fairly straight, with some ups and downs as they went into arroyos and up the other side. The early morning light beamed into the cab from the window behind his head setting whorls of dust motes into do-si-dos.

He turned to Mr. Clyde to ask about gearing down on the hills, but his eyes were closed, the beer car wedged in his crotch.

Ahead in the road Leroy's pickup was like a pilot fish, and Robert was the great white shark, the whale. The big yellow CAUTION! sign across the pickup's grill warned people that a big rig was bearing down on them driven by a man who had a big job to do.

Self-Preservation

Kara is calling them "zombies" behind my back. I caught her mocking the way they stumble along, putting on a show for her giggly pal Emily, arms out sleep-walking, lids half-shut, bumping against the wall like a wind-up toy. "I wuz born somewhere I don't 'member and we had it good back then," she droned.

"Did you notice Burl's missing a finger?" She jumped, startled. "What do you suppose happened? Besides, you'll be there one day."

"Aw, no way! I'll pay somebody to smash my face with a pillow. Or by then they'll have a cure."

She's eleven. My son and daughter-in-law helicopter their kids so when I get the chance, I've tried to expose Kara to life as it's lived by those who can't text or Tweet and don't much care. Earlier today I took Kara on my "rounds" at Autumn Oaks, but I don't mean to imply I'm a doctor. I'm a volunteer ombudsman, and I drop in on residents who otherwise wouldn't get visitors and chat. Mostly, I listen. Sometimes I bring something I know they like or need—a travel pack of Kleenex, say, or a little plastic cup of fruit cocktail. Sometimes they need help finding dentures or glasses or the like, but sometimes I just summon an orderly to change soiled underwear. The staff here don't encourage us to get too hands-on, thank God. At the least my presence tags that resident as someone watched over by an outsider.

Today Kara was supposed to have an active role. Over one shoulder she's slung a pink "Frozen" bookbag containing, along with her phone, a pink-faced spiral, a Bic, and a photocopied sheet with her teacher's suggested questions. Pink's her favorite color—the frames of her glasses are pink plastic. She has a mild case of nystagmus, and her thick lenses magnify green eyes that oscillate minutely. Strangely, this condition hasn't made her shy, though I know pals call her "Owl-ee." She's declared she's up to today's task. Walking away from the parking lot, I tell Kara that Burl was in the Navy during World War II. She says, "Huh! Okay." I add, "But I'm not sure how much he'll remember. Could be not much. Differs from day to day."

I'm wondering not only how much Burl will remember but also how much Kara knows. That war ended well over half a century before she was born, and there've been a slew more since then, some she's heard of, some not. To her anything prior to 2000 or so is ancient history, the Norman Conquest and the Hula Hoop all foreshortened into a single foggy dimension. You're born with a blank slate and maybe that's for the best. The weight of all that woe would discourage the hardiest of starters. So, you take it on as you go along. Then, to judge by the folks here, you start shedding it, and if you have scraps left at the end, they're tucked into your funeral suit.

The complex in East Austin I visit consists of three brick buildings within earshot of a major freeway; there's a building for those who still have the wits and strength to get along without much help, and another building for "assisted living." The third one's for nursing care. If you're here you're most likely in a wheel chair or hobble along with a walker. Maybe you're in your right mind and maybe not. If you are, you're free to roam if you're able; if not, you're locked up so you won't wander. There's a funeral home hardly a gurney-ride away just off 290, so you can move into the East-most block at Autumn Oaks, "graduate" to Assisted Living, then slide on over to Nursing and Memory Care on the West, and eventually get rolled out the back door and down the street.

A high porte-cochere like those on chain motels shades the main entrance, and on our way into the building we pass a gantlet of folks under that cover in wheel chairs, smoking. A couple have oxygen tanks hooked to their chairs and clear plastic lines up their noses. Kara thinks this is funny. Or stupid.

"Don't they know it's not good for them?"

"I guess they're thinking at this point what's the worst could happen?"

"They could die!"

"Well, yeah. True enough. You're right—so don't ever do it."

"Don't worry!"

We sign in at the desk. I ask the young Hispanic fellow there with narrow specs and a loud red necktie about my two residents for today. Burl's about the same, but Eileen had a big adventure yesterday that gave everyone a scare. She's in Assisted Living for now, and "She's got that motor chair. She's hell on wheels," he says. Apparently, she went out at 6 yesterday morning all dressed up–"You know she wears all her best jewelry just to come to lunch"–and drove the chair around East Austin for a couple hours looking for a drug store. When rush hour came, she got lost and scared.

"Didn't she have her phone with her?"

"She forgot it." After a beat, he says, "She forgot where she lives, too, and we had the van out looking for her for an hour and a half. Some guy called in to say he'd had a conversation with her at a Dunkin Donuts and was worried. She told him she thought she lived at 'Falling Leaves' and he figured out what she meant."

Sounds like she's due for a transfer to Memory Care. I know she has no living family—or, at least, none who care she's here. Ten years ago, my mother started out in Nursing and was out the back door within a year. You go down fast once you cross the threshold. Those like me without a mate need someone like me to play the part in the meantime.

There's a big-screen TV in the lobby currently airing a muted "Deal or No Deal" to an audience of patients whose wheel-chairs have been parked in a semi-circle. The color registers are lurid; Howie Mandel's head is the hue and shape of a regulation bas-ketball. On surrounding floral-patterned easy chairs and couches lounge people easily identifiable as visitors—I say "easily" meaning they're too young to be here otherwise. Most don't appear any more alert than the residents nodding off in their wheelchairs. There's discreet email checking among the ambulatory adults. Truth is, it's boring and tedious for everybody to visit the half or wholly demented. Nobody admits that to kids.

Underfoot in the second-floor hall are sage and beige vinyl tiles like those in a hospital or an elementary school. Lunch hour ended fifteen minutes ago, so there's heavy traffic—folks on walkers, canes, scooters. The unmechanized elderly grip the railings along the walls, and you claim the mid-stream by showing you're strong enough to stay vertical. I speak to Mrs. Arnold (she taught typing at the old Austin High School, where my late wife attended), Phillip Nutall (owned a little grocery in San Marcos until H.E.B. moved to his neighborhood), and Vera Underwood, whose history is unknown to me. She often confuses me with her former postman.

"You notice how wide the halls are?"

"Yeah. How come?"

"Wheelchair races."

"That's not true!"

Kara used to believe everything I told her about everything. Now she doesn't believe anything I tell her about anything. I'm waiting for the next phase when she'll have fun chipping in.

"Caught me again."

We reach a bank of glass doors. A keypad's posted on the wall.

"You wanna code us in?"

Happily, she hops to the wall, finger poised. I cup my hand near her ear and whisper, "Three five oh nine." She smirks; she thinks I'm being silly with mock secrecy, but there's a big fellow just on the other side of the glass watching us, and he reads lips. "You see that guy?" She nods. "He'll make believe he wants to hold the door open for you, but he means to come through it soon as we do." I want to add that I know he was a plumbing contractor, an "I bleed orange" Longhorn fan, and he had a yard full of Shelties (pics on his memory wall); I could add it's easy to picture him at the wheel of, say, a black Dodge 1500 diesel Ram with a crew cab, but I refrain—I don't want to overload her with tidbits lest her appetite be glutted before the main course.

"Afternoon, Jack!" I hail him as Kara and I open the door. I thwart his efforts to grab the handle from me and secure it back until it latches.

"Hail-lo!" he booms, and it sounds like Hell no!

Residents this side of the doors never leave the unit unless chaperoned by staff or family. Kara sidles closer. There's a palpable air of misery in this wing—a smile from a patient is rare, and then it probably only means you're mistaken for someone else. Those alert to their surroundings can unnerve you the way they gaze at you without a shred of self-consciousness. The look says they have absolutely no need to worry about what you think. The bald neutrality of their scrutiny is like the stare of an ancient tortoise.

Burl's roommate isn't in. Burl's sitting in the room's one chair fiddling with what looks to be a hearing aid set in his palm. He's bent over with his face down.

"Hey, Burl!" I bellow. Kara jumps. Should've warned her. He looks up. I can always tell instantly whether a resident recognizes me or is only responding to a human voice.

"Hello," he says.

"It's James. You remember?" He nods, being agreeable. They put bibs on them during meals and remove them before they leave the dining room, but his yellow collared shirt has ruddy streaks that might be barbeque sauce. He has wispy white hair, gold-rimmed glasses with lenses smudged by fingerprints, old powder-blue polyester slacks, brown corduroy house slippers. I think when men start wearing house slippers as everyday attire, they're announcing to the world they're giving up all claims to power over themselves.

"This is my granddaughter, Kara." I look at Kara, jerk my head toward Burl, and she leans forward, extending her hand as if Burl might lick it or stick it. He holds his out the way a dog offers you a paw when its master says, "Shake." It's the hand with the ring finger cut back to a rounded nub, and her eyebrows squirm behind those big lenses. She tags his hand and pulls her own back.

I tell her to get out her notebook and pen.

"Burl, Kara would like to talk to you about your experiences in the war. You told me once you were in the Navy. In the Pacific, I think." He was in the Battle of Midway, I recall, and another lesser skirmish near the Solomons, but I want to let him tell it if he can.

I peer down at Kara: okay, your turn! But she looks panicky, terrified. She's got her spiral open and her Bic poised.

"I was born in Mineral Wells. We had it good then."

"You might as well write down everything," I tell her. "You never know." It's plain I'll have to help her.

"You remember the war, Burl?"

He has gone back to the hearing aid. Before we leave, I'll check it.

After a beat, he nods. "We had a fire on board."

"What happened?"

"It was a good town to grow up in."

"What about that fire?"

"Japs."

We plug away for another fifteen minutes, but we don't get much beyond there. He's told me he was a gunner's mate on his cruiser's forward ack-ack so the good news was he had a first-row seat on incoming Zeros and the bad news was he had to watch them plunge right into his battle station. I suppose I can paint a picture for her if he can't.

I lead Kara to Burl's memory board thinking that asking about the photos of his late wife and deceased siblings might jog his recollection. There's a photo of a son in Australia that nobody here seems to know how to contact; to me, that suggests the son doesn't want to be found, and I wonder why. I ask Burl if he was married during the war, though I know he was; I ask him if his brother was overseas (older brother, Army Air Corps, England), but nothing will tug him away from that damned hearing aid.

Finally, I send Kara to the nurse's kiosk for new batteries, and after I coax him to give them up, I clean and service them and reset them in his ears.

"Why's his bed so low?" Kara asks when we're free of the Alzheimer's ward.

"They put them on the floor so they won't fall out and break their hips."

"Seems like that would make them hard to get out of, though."

"That might be part of the reason, too."

After a bit, I add, "You know he said 'Japs.' The Japanese people don't like that term now, but that's what people said back then."

Eileen says, "I worked at this place used to be a radio factory putting together... I forget what we called them." She puts a fist up to her ear.

"Walkie talkies?"

She frowns. "Maybe. Two-time radios."

"Where was it?" asks Kara.

"California. Oh, yes! Things were hopping out there for sure!"

"Was your husband in the war?"

"My husband?" There's a tremolo of fear in her question, as if Kara knows something embarrassing or incriminating that might've slipped her mind. "No, no. I didn't have one then."

"How was it different, then? I mean, not like things now, you know."

"Nobody's going to push you around."

Kara shoots me a glance—help!—but my lip's zipped. "I mean, uh, stuff like you didn't have TV, right?"

"It's right there." She dips her head toward the set on a bookshelf. Her room in Assisted Living is like a studio apartment, though a partition divides her bed space from where we're sitting. Below a small bronzed crucifix on the wall, photos of her at various ages hang in plastic frames. There's a still from an old Western where she had a bit part as a saloon gal, judging by her costume. If you get up close, you can see that years ago some droll impulse provoked her to autograph it to herself: "To Eileen. This was wonderful! Best of Luck! Eileen." Hardly a year or so ago she could tell lively stories on herself in a flirtatious, self-mocking way. I met her when she befriended another of my residents, but soon enough she became someone who needed checking on herself. Now, though, she seems dulled, blunted, that vivacious playfulness lost. I think she knows me, but I'm not sure and don't want to test her.

"I like some shows but a lot of them are just plain silly."

"What's your favorite?"

"That one where they have to guess what things are worth."

Her open hands are resting on the thighs of her black slacks. Her grey hair has been recently washed and permed and maybe tinted, and she's wearing face powder and too much mascara. A big bow of lipstick the hue of a chile pepper is pinned to her lips. These features of her grooming aren't a new development. But when she blinks, squinting, I realize that normally when I've encountered her, she's wearing glasses—of the headlamps variety, from the 80s. Draped over her bosom is a beautiful Navajo squash-blossom necklace, no doubt old and costly, and under it a blue silk blouse with pearl buttons. She likes big brooches, too, gaudy ones with semi-precious stones. She sits erect in the motorized chair, giving off a faint air of condescension and maybe irritation, as if Variety had sent this child cub reporter to interview her. Martinez from the front desk had called up to let her know we were coming. Her tiny feet are clad in bejeweled ballet slippers.

"So what did you do for fun back then?"

Her brow slowly pleats as if she's translating the question.

"During the war," I can't resist inserting. I add, "Listen to the radio, maybe? You once told me you liked 'Fibber McGee and Molly' and 'The Hit Parade.'"

"Oh, yes. There were fellows had them in their cars, you know." There's a beat, a smile. "'Fibber McGee and Molly.'"

Kara pipes up. "How much did you get paid, like when you were working in that radio factory?"

Her head arcs back and to the side and she gives us a low-lidded sidelong glance. We're from the IRS? Or we're out to flim-flam her? "Oh," she says coyly, "We got by." Kara doesn't know that this generation believes it's not polite to ask about a person's money.

Kara dutifully struggles down her list—what was the food like? (We did manage to get the fact of Victory Gardens into the notes). Did people drive cars? How did they get their news? (I helped describe news reels for Kara's benefit). Did you know anybody fighting in the war that you would exchange letters with? Her answers grow increasingly brief or irrelevant. Her gaze wanders, as if she's bored or tired. On previous visits she might have me walk her down to the recreation room where she'd play Cole Porter tunes on the piano and sing. She liked to be read to and wasn't particular about her authors so long as the story "held true" (this, to her, would be John O'Hara and Margaret Mitchell), and she said her greatest irritation about being old was that she couldn't stand up long enough to dance. She was a hatcheck girl at a hotel ballroom in Chicago early in the war and saw all her favorite big-time bands and "song birds" (her word). I've learned she had a child who died of diphtheria, and that she ran away from a man, a handsome Russian boxer, who didn't treat her right. How so? I asked. "You never mind," she said, as if I might be in cahoots.

I intended to ask her about yesterday's jaunt in her motorized chair. My excuse would be that she was supposedly looking for a drug store and I could offer to get what she needs. But now I see it would only embarrass her, and she'd suspect I'd use the information against her. I think she knows what her escapade portends for her future. She'll deny she was lost.

On our way through the lobby, I tell Kara that I'm worried she didn't get enough material from her interviews for an essay–there's a wartime job for a woman (a well-known historical development, yes), and a fire aboard a Navy cruiser caused by a kamikaze attack. But she's walking lightly and looking about with that eager insouciance that spells relief; you'd call it humming if you could hear music.

"Oh, we don't have to write an essay."

"Oh, I thought–"

"What we'll do is Miz Evans will like ask us all the same question from the sheet and we'll all talk about the different answers we got. She said we'll all work together to make a ... a composite person from back then."

"A composite person! Well, that's certainly an ... idea," I say, though what I really mean is the notion scares me. It sounds like assembling someone from spare parts. I've been watching people disappear piece-meal since I started coming here. It's a figurative leprosy, raw chunks of experience falling to the wayside. That it's inevitable, endemic to the human condition, isn't consolation.

We move through the doors and under the smokers' awning. It's well after 2 by now, so the after-lunch bunch has gone in to nap, and the smoker's station by the ash urns is femaled by a brace of orderlies in rumpled turquoise scrubs.

"I used to smoke," I say. "A pack a day at least."

"Really?"

"Yeah. I quit when your dad was born."

"Huh!"

"Yes. And I also have to admit it's not much fun for me to be here, either. It's boring and it makes me think of things I don't want to think about. But, you know, when your great-grandmother was here, a lot of people helped me take care of her. So, I'm just returning the favor."

Kara cocks her head, squinting at me against the sunlight. She has no idea why I'm saying this.

"I can also tell you stories about Miz Pazuros that you can use, even though looks like she has forgotten them herself, okay?" If not use, at least know. "Anyway, stay tuned," I add.

It's a good thirty minutes or so through traffic from Autumn Oaks to Kara's home in Westlake. Though I know she's dying to dig out her phone and plug in her earbuds, I force her to acknowledge my existence by monologuing. I tell her about my adventures as a kid with water-balloon fights, Halloween pranks, the time three of us stole lumber from a construction site for a homecoming float and were shot at by a nightwatchman, about how a girl broke my heart and so I joined the Marines, about how her grandmother and I fled Nixon's Amerika to live in Mexico before Kara's father was born, about my first wife, the one before Kara's grandmother. I kept thinking Come on! You need to write this all down, but I knew in the end these vignettes, these parts of my life, could be saved only by her memory.

Suitors

On Monday after Easter of 1937, Ellen Hudson was working at a Baptist bookstore in Birmingham. She was shelving new arrivals when her boss, Roberta, passed her an envelope. "For you," she said with a sly smile. Roberta returned to the register where a customer waited. Outside along Eighteenth Street South, an afternoon breeze sent azalea blossoms aswirl like red confetti.

The ecru envelope came from Roberta's son's stationery. On the back flap, Arial letters in a deep burnt umber:

Timothy Michael Boyd
School of Medicine
Tulane University
New Orleans, La.

Ellen suspected the contents were very personal and that maybe Roberta was aware of them. Not wanting her reaction witnessed, Ellen put it in her purse. As she was scurrying out the door at closing time, Roberta looked up, brows cocked in a mimed Yes? So?, but Ellen tossed her a cheery, "See you tomorrow!"

She often walked to save money, but today she needed meditative space and took the bus to the YWCA on 20th Street. The Y was cheap and safe, and the Christian imprimatur satisfied her grandmother's standards for an unmarried woman, particularly one with a streak of iconoclasm borne of reading Dorothy Parker, Victorian female novelists, and Emily Dickinson (*Some keep the Sabbath going to church—I keep it staying at home...*). Since Ellen stopped writing the devotional verse she'd penned in high school and had turned to irony or cynicism as her preferred mode, her grandmother no longer fully trusted her decisions.

Her grandmother's husband had been very on-again off-again in their lives, as had Ellen's father, so the women had made sure to get educated sufficiently to be teachers or clerks. Her grandmother worked for the Southern Baptist's sprawling publishing ventures in Nashville as a secretary and proof-reader, and Ellen's mother had typed and charmed her way into an executive assistantship at Nashville's tony Colemere Club. The grandmother, Blanche, wrote ferociously Christian verse, and she had paid for Ellen's college at an institution exclusively for women in East Tennessee. The money lasted two years before the Depression bit it deep after nibbling at it. Blanche had found Ellen this roving temporary job in the Baptist bookstore chain, although the salary barely covered her necessities. Her current assignment began in January and would last another month.

The ride offered the privacy to read the letter, but she left it in her purse. She guessed Tim had written it last night before going back to New Orleans this morning. They'd spent most of yesterday, Easter Sunday, together. She'd met him through Roberta in January when he was home for the holidays.

Five minutes after their meeting at the store, he'd asked her to a movie.

When she hesitated, he smiled (winningly, she admitted) and added, as if this were an added incentive, "I was thinking *The Good Earth*. Did you read the book?"

"Yes."

"I haven't finished the book yet. I don't get as much time as I'd like to read anything but a textbook. You could tell me if they've done it justice."

She hesitated to reply because she didn't like events to jump up in her face before she could throw up her arms. It was also a disconcerting novelty to have some other fellow's attention. She and Will Parker had been paired since high school, but he was now working in Corpus Christi, Texas, and, although they'd written while separated during the last two school years—he was at Vanderbilt—lately his letters had disturbingly stopped coming.

She felt uneasy to be asked out by another man, but Tim's mother—her boss—was within earshot, and simply going to a movie seemed harmless. No reason to feel guilty. And not so incidentally, Tim was very handsome. He was tall, with thick, curly black hair and gray eyes. His gaze was earnest but faintly wounded. She felt complimented by his good looks. She'd agreed to the movie, thinking just this once won't hurt. But then a few times he came to the store at noon and insisted on taking her and Roberta to lunch—knowing, Ellen supposed, that both couldn't leave at once—and Roberta would decline and shoo them out the door. Ellen had felt a bit manipulated, but it was gratifying (and economical) to save her tuna sandwich for dinner and be treated to a filling blue-plate special at a cafe where chattering office workers made intimacy impossible, thankfully.

Tim was cheerful, funny, telling anecdotes about medical school in which he was the innocent dupe of pranks, and to Ellen he was unfailingly chivalrous with doors and chairs and coats. To questions about her family, she gave sanitized answers. At what point, she wondered, should she say she was "spoken for," was how people put it. But wouldn't that be presumptuous? The more she sorted through her feelings, the more hurt she was at Will's odd silence, and a small part of her wanted recompense.

Tim made the train trip from New Orleans more often than you'd think normal. And with each visit came an invitation to their Methodist church and dinner with the family at their spacious Victorian two-story home that boasted a favorite architectural feature of Ellen's—a wide and deep front porch populated by white wicker rockers and side tables, potted ferns. There were porcelain Chinese vases and Persian carpets, and the Sunday meals were catered by a restaurant whose owner was a family friend. Ellen hoped to have such a house someday. Knowing no one in Birmingham, her loneliness eased in the visits to the Boyd family's home.

Tim said, while driving her back to the Y in the family's yacht-like Packard, "My Mom really likes you."

Ellen said, "Well, I like her, too."

He added, "Julie thinks you're super. My Dad says you're cute as a bug."

That had been said before, and it irked her. It implied a generosity on the speaker's part.

"Oh, well, they're really nice."

She hoped that was all, but he went on. "And I really like you, too!" He laughed when he said it, as if it were only the punchline to a joke he'd set up, and she felt off the hook.

"Well, it's nice to be liked so much."

The truth was, disturbingly, distressingly, she'd come to like him as well. She liked him enough to be afraid of liking him more. Prior to meeting Tim, she had felt that her heart was settled, but now Will's silence made her worry about him and about her own feelings, and her confidence in Will, in them, was growing shaky. To suddenly find that Tim could arouse her interest was a little thrilling but also frightening, promising in equal measures the rosy pleasures of infatuation and the torment of feeling unfaithful.

From her mother's and grandmother's lives, she'd learned caution. Even as she was here in Birmingham working, her father was galivanting about from race track to race track while her mother dutifully rose daily to ride a bus to her job. He'd call collect to say he'd been robbed and needed her mother to wire him money to get home. Her grandmother called him a "common varmint," though her own husband sporadically went missing for months without warning.

To most young women, Tim would be "a really great catch." Ellen wasn't sure how she'd rate, though she supposed it wouldn't be high. She had to support herself, whereas Tim never asked what things cost and still got a generous allowance at 23 ("as long as I'm in school," he explained). Mr. Boyd's stake in newspapers and radio had sheltered the family from a downturn, and Roberta worked just because she "liked to be out in the world."

It was refreshing to be with Roberta when she showed a rebellious side. Roberta seemed wearily dutiful about the obligatory church attendance sometimes, saying to Ellen once as she was tugging fiercely to fit a white glove to her left hand, "Hate these!" She smiled wryly at Ellen. "Lucky you, you've got no hubby to appease." Ellen laughed. "I left my gloves in Nashville along with my grandmother's scrutiny."

"Someday I'll show up at church wearing slacks and saddle shoes."

"I will if you will."

They laughed.

"Or maybe I won't go at all."

"Oh! Now you're scaring me."

As for that catered Sunday dinner, Ellen learned that it annoyed Mr. Boyd that Roberta spent money that way, even if from her manager's salary.

"I guess it saves time," Ellen offered. "It'd be hard to have the whole family go to church and then for you to make a big meal, too."

"Well, in the first place, I can't cook worth a damn, and in the second place I hate it."

When they were alone in the store, Roberta often brewed tea and insisted that they sit in her office to "take a load off." Roberta seemed to want a confidante, and Ellen liked Roberta's candor. Roberta said Julie was a "very disappointing child" because she "lacked substance." Julie was too pretty for her own good, and she presumed that would be her most powerful asset.

"I told her the most beautiful girl in my senior class slit both wrists and bled to death in the family's bathtub."

"You did?"

"Yeah. Probably stepped over a line there. But I was making a point that beauty won't get you very far."

"Oh, I don't know," said Ellen. "I've seen men fall all over themselves to open a door for some dish when they'll close it in a plain girl's face."

"True. And I know my children are good-looking. They got it from Boyd. But he thinks his good looks are just part of his business portfolio. Whether it moves a woman seems immaterial. Now, Tim doesn't even know that he's that handsome, I think. It's like he was born with virtuoso musical talent but has never picked up an instrument."

"Huh!" said Ellen.

"One more gripe then I'll shut up. It disturbs me that Julie will not read a single word of anything not assigned by a teacher. Can you imagine?"

"No," said Ellen. "I really can't."

Roberta said that she's been poking away at writing a novel for years.

"What's it about?" Ellen asked with genuine curiosity.

Roberta grinned. "It's a satire on the modern American family."

"That sounds juicy."

Roberta laughed. "Sometimes after I write the racy passages, I have to take a cold shower. Boyd gets the benefit, though, believe me."

"Oh, well, now I really do want to read it."

Roberta waved her off. "It's not ready for exposure. Poor thing's too delicate, might wilt."

They often smoked Roberta's cigarettes. ("Boyd hates it," she said.)

Roberta said that Tim had scads of talent and that she believes that deep in his heart of hearts he wants to be an artist but Boyd wouldn't have that for a minute.

"Really? He doesn't want to be a doctor?"

"Oh, he's playing along. He'd be a good one, don't you think?"

"Well, he is smart and seems to care about people."

"Has he told you he's doing a pen-and-ink portrait of you?"

"Really?! He's never mentioned it."

"He hasn't finished it. It's already much better than those he did of that ninny he was way too sweet on in high school. Jesus, she annoyed me no end. Never stopped talking and yet never said a damn thing."

Ellen wanted to ask more, a lot more, but held her tongue. She had finished her cigarette and wanted to wash her hands and rinse her mouth, but the store was empty and Roberta was apparently not sated.

"So what about you?"

"What about me?"

"You won a poetry prize."

"Oh, that was in high school. I still write, though."

"That's good. What's your long-term goal?"

After a moment, Ellen said, "Nobody's ever asked me that."

"Haven't you ever asked you that?"

"Not in so many words."

Roberta stared at her in mock dismay, nodding as if to say, yes, yes, come on! and Ellen felt that her silence was miserly.

"Well," she said at last. "I have what I guess you could call longings."

"Aha! Now we're getting somewhere!"

"I want to see some cities in Europe, look at some great art especially in Italy, and I want to see the redwood forests in California and hike part of the Appalachian Trail. And I want to have enough money to have my own car someday. Maybe something sporty."

"Laudable! You and Nancy Drew! No patter of tiny feet, a cottage with a picket fence, and a rose arbor blah blah blah?"

Ellen blushed. Will's face popped to mind. That question demanded an answer. Ellen waved vaguely and joked, "Maybe. The rose arbor, anyway."

"You know what I like about you?" declared Roberta. "Your seriousness. Your quiet watchfulness. A person gets the feeling the gears are always turning." She tapped her forehead.

"I guess so. Sometimes it's a curse."

"In what way?"

"Oh, I think and think and the chance for applying whatever I might decide has long passed."

"Hamletta."

Ellen laughed. "Yes."

Knowing Roberta was a bracing experience. She seemed ultra-modern, stylishly Bohemian, though toned down for a "lady" in the South married to a traditional man of means. But though Roberta played the rebel in their tete-a-tetes, when she gloved up on Sundays with her arm looped through the crook of her husband's elbow and was chatting with pals in the congregation, futzing with Tim's tie and nudging Julie to sit up straight, the rebel Roberta faded, overtaken by the persona she otherwise might've mocked.

Yesterday–Easter Sunday–Ellen had almost declined the invitation knowing that Roberta and Julie would wear new frocks, and she had nothing but everyday clothes in her wardrobe. But they'd find her absence peculiar, and if her grandmother learned she missed an Easter service, Ellen would never hear the last of it. Also, as she'd hoped, the after-service meal had been swooningly bountiful, and, although she tried to resist from fear of making a bad impression, she'd eaten herself almost comatose. She'd also had two glasses of something pink and fizzy and cold. Not her very first wine, but she'd only touched alcohol since leaving the Baptist fold in Nashville. The Boyds served it to all at the table regardless of age.

After lunch, Tim drove her to Avondale Park. It was a warm and breezy afternoon, and the ball fields echoed the pok of knocked baseballs and shouted cheers. Tim had planned on their strolling through the park's new rose garden then sitting in a gazebo overlooking the pond, but as they were arriving, a brief shower scattered the ball players, and Easter Sunday picknickers claimed the gazebos.

They sat in the Packard with the doors open to smell the moist floral air that had swept through the trees during the shower. It was pleasant, and she was still full from the Easter feast and buoyant from the wine. She and Tim chatted about his classes, her work. "So tell me, just between us—" He grinned. "How's my mom to work for?"

"She's a decent boss, knows when to be helpful and when to butt out."

"Mom says you two just chat away like old pals." He chuckled. "I'm guessing that means she yaks at you and you politely listen."

"Oh, no! Much more than that! She's... wonderful to talk to, Tim!"

"It's nice she listens to you, anyway."

He craned his arm over the seat, reached into the well behind him, and retrieved a large manila folder. He passed it to her.

"I want to show you something."

She undid the string binder, reached and slid out a large piece of sketch paper. The portrait. Maybe it was the wine, but it seemed she'd never looked that beautiful. It was stunning, and it embarrassed her to be so in love with herself to look at it. Was this how he saw her?

"It's... My God!" She favored him with an admiring gaze. "You are really, really good, Tim!"

He shrugged. "It's the subject."

"Don't be ridiculous. How'd you get to be this good?"

"Well, now, don't go overboard. I had a few lessons."

"Can I have it?"

He hesitated for an instant and she later thought he wanted to keep it, but then, that day, he said, "Sure! I'm already working on another one."

"You have a real gift. How long have you been doing it?"

He shifted in his seat and looked off to the ball fields a moment. "I had rheumatic fever when I was twelve and had to spend five months mostly in bed." He turned to her. "Not many people know about that, Ellen, I mean people who don't know me from when I was a kid. I don't talk about it much." He shrugged and cleared his throat. "I guess no fellow wants to be seen as sickly."

"I can understand."

"Anyway, I read a lot, and I started drawing everything I saw. Mom got excited and hired a tutor, and she gave me a lot of pointers."

"Roberta thinks that you'd really like to be an artist and not a doctor."

He sighed, turned, and passed her a weary look. "I know. It's a bee in her bonnet. You'd think having a son in med school would thrill most mothers, right? But she likes to think of herself as someone who aids and abets people's 'real self' as she puts it, even when they deny and resist it."

"So you want to be a doctor?"

"Well, I spent months in bed feeling pretty lousy. Every now and then some kid's mom would make them come cheer me up. Oh, gosh, I felt so sorry for them. It's really boring to visit a sick person, almost as boring as being one weeks on end. And you know, kids have no patience for that. Rheumatic fever can knock you down, so I never felt well enough to be decent company. When you're sick and it seems as if there's no end to it, you start to feel you don't belong to the rest of the world. You're an outsider. You're missing out, been cut out. Being sick that way is lonely."

When Ellen reached to pat his shoulder, he chuckled, took her hand, squeezed it, let it go. "I'm not saying this to extract some pity. I felt plenty sorry for myself without any help. But I started to think that this could be a useful experience. I could grow up to be someone who not only understood what it was like to be sick that way but also to have the know-how to ease that pain. Maybe I'd be one up on a doctor who had no idea about that. When you're in the grip of an illness like that, that's all you are to yourself and to the world. I know what that feels like. So, yes, I want to be a doctor."

"Oh," said Ellen. "That was... Have you ever told her this?"

He laughed.

"How about your father?"

"Oh, he's fine with having a son be a doctor. We're on good terms, but we don't talk about things that are... tricky, I guess you could say."

He turned to peer at her intensely. "I feel like I can talk to you, Ellen."

"I'm really happy to be talked to," Ellen said hurriedly, her own gaze skittering away. "I miss my mother and grandmother even though I don't always want to listen when they talk to me." She was trying to joke her way out of a dangerous approach of intimacy. She felt off-balance, maybe from the wine, she thought.

He smiled indulgently. "Anyway, the sketching–when I started doing it while I was locked up, it just took me away. That's what it still does. I don't need to be an artist and sell or show anything. If I sketch for an hour, when I quit and look up, it's like I had a kind of emotional siesta. It's weird. I'm calm but feel really alert and rested."

"Oh, I know! I'm the same about writing poems! Not just like being emptied of something but also being filled, too!"

They rounded out their day by seeing *Nothing Sacred* with Carole Lombard and Frederick March - Tim liked screwball comedies–and later sat in the dark parked in front of the Y. Despite his laughter during the movie, Tim seemed moody, preoccupied. He said he'd be graduating in a few weeks, that if he was lucky, he'd land an internship at a good hospital. He'd wanted to stay "close by," but he'd had to widen his search.

"I guess you'll be going back to Nashville?"

"Maybe. I might be sent somewhere else."

"Uncertain futures," he sighed. "I don't much care for uncertain futures."

He walked her to the door of the Y where, for the first time, he bent close and kissed her chastely on the lips. That startled her, though later she thought she should've expected it. She felt suddenly shaky. It had been so long since anyone, let alone a man, had come this close and touched her—bringing his heat, his scent, the pressure of his leg against hers, so she had to tilt into the doorframe for support. Unlike Will's sort of drowsy, languid kisses, Tim's peck was so abrupt and brief that she'd not had time to accept or reject it. She saw he'd been trying to acknowledge an imminent shift in their circumstances that would change their standing, but she didn't know how to respond. Later, in her room, she was so unhappy with herself she cried. She could see the signs in Tim—his affection toward her had grown. *I can talk to you* was such a flashing indicator. And her spirit had leapt to meet his in an involuntary spasm. So dangerous. And because she was so lonely, she knew. She could see the signs in herself, too.

It was Will's own fault. No, not really. She wasn't being fair. Not fair to Tim to keep mum about Will, not fair to Will for her to encourage Tim's warmth by being friendly. Tim had been only an acquaintance at first, a lunch or movie companion, not even a "friend" except only in the loosest sense, and that was safe territory. She'd had no reason to feel guilty, no reason he should know her relationship with Will, so long as he was merely her employer's son looking for a pal on visits home. But that reasoning was so flimsy! After all, born and raised here, he doubtless had friends he could spend time with. So why choose her?

Because her company meant more.

She tugged the portrait out of the manila sleeve but couldn't bear to look at it closely and slid it back. Who is that girl?

Tim's story moved her deeply, and being moved deeply by another fellow so appealing was frightening—it brought confusion, uncertainty. To imagine Tim as that boy in his bed day after day, lonely and enduring awkward visits from pals that brought no comfort and only embarrassment—it broke her heart, really, made her feel about him in a way that she didn't wish to feel about anyone else but Will.

Why hadn't she heard from him? His silence was a torment.

In the lobby of the Y, she checked her mail cubby and found it disappointingly, disturbingly, empty. In her room, she set the purse containing Tim's unopened letter on her desk chair. She changed into old dungarees, sneakers, and a rag-soft cotton blouse. Went down the hall to the shower room to wash her face, neck, arms, and hands. She made a cup of tea with the hot plate on her dresser. She thought about a cigarette but had none. Chocolate. Dark chocolate would help, too.

Finally, she sat at her desk and opened the envelope that Roberta had given her, took a breath, drew out the note.

Dear Ellen,

There was so much I wanted to say before I left but I never could get it out—It's probably best, though, because you might not of believed me, this soon, anyway. I can hardly believe it myself, that I came so soon to have such a strong attachment.

I can't remember enjoying myself as much as I do when I've been with you—I have never developed an affinity for anyone so deeply and quickly as I have for you - it surprises me - you've been in my mind constantly ever since that first day. What I wanted to say was that I want you more than anything—I'm sorry to not say those things out loud to you.

I'll be leaving New Orleans in June and the aspiring doctor in me hopes for an internship at a hospital with the prestige and resources that will launch a career - and I'm at that point in my adult life when it's time to think of taking on the joys and responsibilities of a wife and family too.

What I most wanted to say was will you be a part of my future and what I hoped for was to hear you say yes.

Love,
Tim

134

Her face flushed suddenly. Her heart was pounding; she felt breathless.

The note was a proposal. No wonder Roberta was so... smirky when she handed it over this morning. Tim had confided in her.

But was it a proposal? No ring. No "Will you marry me?" So being "part of my future" gave both a way to save face. She could pretend it meant corresponding by long-distance until a future catalyst called for a wedding or a rift or drifting apart. That wasn't what he really meant, she knew. She could sympathize with how much courage it took to go as far as he did without encouragement. She'd not been forward, had she? She would never want to be coy and hint at things that may or not be true or may or not come to pass.

But she'd not been honest, either, had she?

She and Will were... Were what? He'd said "I love you," and she'd not had the gumption to say it back. She needed to be sure of his feelings, but now she didn't know what sort of test he'd have to pass to prove them. He'd said it more than once, and her response had been a hug or a joke ("Silly boy!") and a chuck on his cheek or a peck on the lips. But she'd felt it, for sure. Oh, what had she been waiting for?

Despite months of separation broken only by holiday reunions, she believed neither had spent time with anyone who might erode their bond. She hadn't, anyway. Up to now, anyway. She just "knew" Will wanted to marry her, though he'd never said anything definite. He'd say that it costs money to set up housekeeping, and his family would never think it's right for a couple to take that step without standing on their own feet, especially when families were strapped already. She got the impression that money was the obstacle to his proposing. And she was too shy and cautious to say, "Now we're both working, but we could both work in the same city," because that would be like a proposal from her.

Their holiday reunions had been vital to renewing their bond. Except for this past Christmas. She longed to have five minutes of that evening back. Her sorry mood. And she couldn't blame it all on having her period, just being broody as well, and the spat with her mother after she'd given her father money because "everybody deserves a nice Christmas." Like he was one of her children and not her husband—or Ellen's father. And it all spilled over onto Will.

Just to be practical—she was 22. How many offers would she get? The collective voice of female wisdom might say, *Okay, so maybe you don't "love" love Tim right now the way you feel about*

Will, but you can imagine how easily that could happen with a fellow so good and true. Can't you? And aren't you halfway there? And okay so he kisses like he's in grammar school, but maybe that just means he's had no practice. He's a polite and handsome fellow with a great family who likes you and, to be crass, they've got lots of bucks! No more tuna sandwiches! No more worn-out underwear! No more standing for half an hour in a packed and smelly bus on a rainy day!

But men with money? They might not always have it or even spend it on you and your children. Her grandmother's father had owned a popular restaurant in Nashville, but he got too ambitious and bought into a resort hotel in the mountains northeast of town. He took on a big debt, but then he promptly keeled over from a stroke. Her grandmother had been 12, with three younger siblings. One of whom, a sister, years later had her husband swallow strychnine just as she was giving birth to their third child, and he took a week to die.

The women in her family were cursed with either horrible luck or an appalling inability to judge the character of men they chose. It made Ellen very protective of her feelings.

"Oh, Will!" she sighed. "Damn it all! Where the devil are you??!"

****

Poem Ellen began on the back of an invoice found in a drawer:

Delayed
Delayed:
A little anger
Then too late
For love to be dismayed -
Oh, wait!

Delayed:
A little love -
And then too late
For love to be repaid
Why wait?

****

Yesterday afternoon, while Ellen was with Tim on Easter Sunday, Will was writing in a Big Chief tablet using a yellow pencil with a #2 lead.

Dear Ellen,

    Boy, howdy, this is the first time in a good while I haven't been so dog-tired that I can sit down and write you a decent account of myself. (Not true, really just my vow to resist making a pest of myself by flooding your mail box with my sorrowful love-struck mash notes like I did last fall that seemed to get me nowhere, poor me, and am now surrendering to the power of your doggone charm... Hmm, said the critic—too many dogs there!)

    Uncle Kirby's back on the wagon and that's to the good but I don't think he'll have the wherewithal to get me back to Vandy next fall but we'll see. Homco pays pretty well, so chances might be that if I eat day old bread and rat cheese all week, I'll save enough and stay afloat by working the slop line at the dormitory again.

    "Quit it," said Frank.

    "What?"

    "That thing with your heel, you know, like you're doing some kind of hillbilly dance. It's disturbing my reading."

    "How much attention does a shoot-em-up take, anyway."

    It was hard to sit still sometimes.

    Oh, thinking about you is scattering my poor brain! I'm cursed with a roomie here at Betty B's boarding house, and he's lying on his bunk reading a Western, and I just wanna kick him out so's I can dream about you in peace or sob my eyes out in heart-break (just joshing). Now and again, he'll stop reading and carve on his toenails with a Bowie knife. He's a pain to live with, but it cuts my rent in half and he's a good man to have on the other end of a chunk of pipe you have to tote clear across a field.

    I hope your job in Birmingham's going well! I haven't heard from you but once since you started, so for all I know you're off to Knoxville or eloped with an Arab sheik or a baseball star! (Sure hope not!) I could tell when I saw you Christmas that maybe you didn't welcome the burden of answering my letters, but I assure you that now I'm not in school and am a workaday fellow, I don't have time to pester you, so you can read this one without feeling obliged to match it word for word! I promise!

    Now I'm going to wax nostalgic. If there is one thing I want to remember most about my Senior year, it is this: the skit on stunt night. Why? Because I remember you in your flowing dress, and wasn't there something in your hair? I remember too that I was with you more than ever before during all those rehearsals. And all our picnics in Percy Warner Park with the Echo staff and how we always kind of faded into the woodlands (and not the woodwork) so we could amble holding hands. And somebody's luscious lips float in my mind, I wonder whose?

You know, when I'm with you I get a funny choked feeling. Is it noticeable? I also remember a Dramatics class, a purple (?) wool dress with a purple and white collar that fitted closely about your neck. Forgive me, also flowers for Senior Day. Speaking of flowers, you remember this poem from Poe?

"A green isle in the sea, love,
A fountain and a shrine
All wreathed with fairy fruits and flowers
And all the flowers were mine."

See, I haven't forgotten how much you love your poetry, you crazy little rascal. I'm in a bind here writing you 'cause I'm not sure you want to hear all the goopy stuff that's in my heart and head about you - we both don't want me to embarrass me!– and what I do day to day is pretty darned boring to tell. I guess I could inventory my muscle aches and bruises and scratches just to squeeze a tear from your beautiful brown eyes for a poor doomed admirer.

So maybe a little more verse just to show you I ain't no hick. Let's say I'm tired (I am): "My head aches, and a drowsy numbness pains my sense, as though of hemlock I had drunk or emptied some dull opiate to the brain" Keats—Ode to a Nightingale. Cost Uncle Kirby $126 for me to learn that, so why not use it? Not being able to see you makes me want to get drunker than the lords in "The Eve of St. Agnes." (Another $126!)

I'd much rather talk to you now than writing. First, I'd tell you how crazy you are. Then I'd tell you how glad I am. Then in my shy, boyish way, how much I care.

Should he add "to send or not to send, that is the question"? Another $126. A shame that tuition hadn't bought an easy answer. He'd written several such letters in the past three months but hadn't mailed them.

At Christmas, the more he showed his feelings, the more she withdrew. She'd been at Carson-Newman all fall, and he at Vandy, and he hadn't seen her since Thanksgiving. When he went to her grandmother's house the day after Christmas for a supper of leftovers, he wanted desperately to be alone with her. Her mother tied him up asking about his schooling—it impressed her that he was at Vanderbilt—and he couldn't bring himself to tell Ellen with her grandmother present that he had to leave school and work in Texas. It was such a recent development that he hadn't had the chance to write. It was bad news, as it put him hundreds of miles from her.

She'd already told him that she was coming back to Nashville because they couldn't afford a school where room and board was an added burden. He'd hoped to still be at Vanderbilt and she'd be home in Nashville for the spring.

He'd have sworn she was avoiding him that evening. She kept busy helping in the kitchen and was nanny to younger cousins from Huntsville. When she went to the bathroom, he slipped away from the parlor and waited (maybe to her it would be lurked?) in the hall. When she came out, she embraced him wordlessly but didn't have her whole heart in it. When he tried to kiss her neck, she shrugged him off and whispered, "No! Don't. Not here."

The next day, he was on the train for Corpus. After Ellen got to Birmingham, she wrote him to describe her new job and her new employer. Then she apologized for her coldness that night. She said that she really cared for him despite her moods. She was upset that day because of family things. "If anybody has my heart, it's you, Will," she wrote.

If anybody. She was always a mystery. He did not know for sure what the heck she felt about him. He was afraid his heart was in for a bruising.

Sunday afternoon's when we're off, so when the weather's good, we usually go to the beach or to Cole Park Pier. Frank likes to lolly-gag at the ladies, but I swear I keep my sights set on a certain poetess, and you know who. It's raining today, and there's no sun. I bet you could make a poem about sitting in a room on a rainy Sunday afternoon missing a certain someone.

Tomorrow we've got a big job hauling a pump jack down to Alice.

Oh, why would she care? The more he wrote, the sillier he sounded. It helped to remember that he didn't have to send this. Red pen it down to Miss you! Wish you were here!

"Hey, Frank. How do you rate with that gal in Sugarland?"

"What gal?"

"I guess that answers it."

"So you writing to your honey-pie?"

"Well, I'm about to. Maybe."

"You're a fellow with a lot of maybes."

Epitaph: *Will was a fellow with a lot of maybes.*

He'd told her in so many ways. Maybe too many. (Another maybe, Will?) Since their Christmas get-together, he'd decided that his ardor had scared her off, made her wary. He'd been too pushy, maybe (!!), and the old saw about sweeping a gal off her feet didn't apply to one who was afraid of being airborne, you could say.

139

But could be that in his silence he'd faded out of her mind and whatever corner of her heart he'd managed to colonize, and agonizing about it was pathetic and pointless. Frank would say There's other fish in the sea.

But, as the poetess put it, *Hope is the thing with feathers.* (ka-ching!) He could also say *nothing ventured, nothing gained* and *faint heart never wins fair lady,* but he didn't need a college diploma to know that.

****

In lieu of a letter, Will sent a telegram.

HOME FOR MED EMER STOP RETURN CORPUS VIA BIRMGHM WED STOP HOPE TO CALL STOP

A tremor like a chill shook her. She sat at her desk and parsed the words. Medical emergency? Will's parents were in good health but anything could happen to anybody any time. Her grand-mother's father, at the height of his powers and ambition, collapsing and dragging everything into his grave.

He's returning to Texas on Wednesday? The day after tomorrow—would he go back to Corpus so soon if the situation was dire? Probably not.

Wouldn't you likely go from Nashville west to Memphis, maybe?

Did that mean he's going out of his way to see her?

And "hope" to call? He might not have a chance to step off the train and call? In that case, the stop here wouldn't be because he'd fashioned his itinerary to see her.

Or did "hope" only mean "I hope you will/can answer."

Oh, Tim, I too hate "uncertain futures."

Monday night she hardly slept. Will's grinning face kept poking its way into her awareness, and she let his absence sink into her core after having pushed it out for months.

Walking to work Tuesday morning, she fretted over asking Roberta for Wednesday afternoon off. She'd avoided her boss the past week for fear Roberta would talk about Tim's note. She had put off answering him because she knew that being honest about Will would end Tim's companionship, but she also didn't want to overtly encourage him or take advantage of his innocence. She waffled. Made several starts, tore them up.

It was hard to walk into Roberta's office knowing that Will's

140

presence was why she needed time off.

Her boss was punching buttons on a calculator, but looked up when Ellen walked in. Roberta held up a finger, peered closely at a paper for a beat, then smiled.

"What's up?" She waved to the empty chair by the desk, but Ellen pretended the gesture hadn't registered.

She asked Roberta for Wednesday afternoon off. She added, "A friend is visiting from out of town."

"How nice! I know you must get lonely here."

Tuesday night she lay awake in a stew of speculation. She agonized over her behavior at Christmas. Being reticent was deep in her nature, and it was possible that Will took that to signal an absence of tender feelings, and he'd looked elsewhere for someone better. That could explain his silence. He'd given up on her. He was a decent sort who'd deliver bad news face to face, he'd feel he owed her that. They'd been pals since junior year, then more since then, but what? His letters were mushy, boyish, a bit silly in a way that made the feelings expressed seem too casually come by to be wholly credible, dependable. Her deadbeat dad had just that charm, so glib he could talk the food right off your plate and onto his.

Skinny Boy. Her pet name. Shards of memory tumbled through her waking hours. His older brother gravitated toward their father, but Will was his mother's favorite. She was a petite, undereducated chatterbox who'd never worked a day in her life, and Will's father was a bonds salesman when the bottom fell out. They seemed to limp along now. Ellen was never sure of what Will's mother thought of her and her family—Florence was too Southern "sweet" to openly be a snob—but Ellen's circumstances as a child and granddaughter of women more or less abandoned to shift for themselves made her skittish and self-conscious, and she feared she never made a good enough impression.

Skinny Boy had a wiry frame clad in springy musculature, big-boned, and always moving, bobbing, bouncing, endlessly energetic. He swam, played volleyball, tennis, badminton, and he boxed as a welterweight. She saw one Golden Gloves match. He and an opponent pummeled each other mercilessly for three rounds, bashing noses, their faces intent, ferocious, awash in blood, but, later, he and the fellow laughed and joked like best pals. How that violence wasn't anger was a mystery.

Will kissed her like he was slowly savoring a most delicious dessert. The first kiss happened in her grandmother's back yard under a willow whose green drapery enclosed and hid them. She trembled and shivered—it was like a rhapsodic spasm of delightful flu, and it scared her no end, the power of it over her senses.

And he loved dancing, but not a fancy ballroom waltz or tango or foxtrot. (She'd had absolutely no practice.) He was keen on the Charleston, the Lindy Hop, the Shag—anything so vigorous that it was like calisthenics set to music, and her role was to stand nearby and bend her knees up and down while he hijinked all around her. She razzed him about it.

Once she asked him what he saw in her. He flushed deep red.

"Okay, uh, well. Since you asked, mm. When I look at you, I just want to keep staring and staring, no particular part, mind you, just all of you or only a bit, it doesn't matter. You know that photo I have in my wallet—sometimes I just gawk until I'm paralyzed, which is downright inconvenient sometimes."

"I have others where I'm ugly as mud I can give you."

"And also I like that you're smart and quiet and listen to people and think before you say something. I need an earnest person in my life, somebody with—what's that word, gravitas?—yeah, that."

And I need your cheerful optimism, she thought.

"I like reading your poetry, too." He grinned. "I keep waiting to read one about me."

She laughed. "You'd be the last I'd show it to."

"Oh, gosh! A fellow could take that so many ways."

"Well, don't worry about it."

"Also, you're tender-hearted."

"I am?"

"Yeah. Robson's spaniel?"

"Well, they left me in charge of that poor animal."

"That pup only had a sprained paw but you carried on like he was on his deathbed. I got a little jealous, to tell the truth."

"If you sprained your paw, I'd tend to you, too."

"I'll work on it."

Tender-hearted? The secret's out, she guessed. He knows it, anyway. Her sensitivity often made her feel like an unshelled turtle or snail, and her armor had to consist of caution. Truth be told, she was more tender-hearted toward animals and birds and flowers and trees than toward most humans.

In the morning, everything in her skimpy wardrobe was too old, too big, too small, too dark, too light, too loose, too tight. She had a light blue cotton dress patterned with small flowers, an A-line skirt that fell mid-calf, with small puff sleeves, a Peter Pan collar, and seven round covered buttons going up the front like pearls. It was old, and therefore too girlish, she knew, but Will liked it.

Hair up or down? Lipstick, yes. Nothing more, okay?

She asked the desk clerk to telephone her at the store if anyone should look for her or call. She arrived at work just as Roberta was unlocking the front door.

"Oh, my! Don't you look nice!"

"Oh, well, just needed a change."

"Are you and your friend going somewhere special?"

Ellen suspected the question had a subtext. "Oh, I don't know. Such a nice day—we'll most likely go to the park and walk around, maybe window-shop."

Frustrated by the uncertainty of Will's arrival, she leeched off her anxiety by rearranging heavy book boxes in the storage room, even cleaning the bathroom, keeping one ear open in case Roberta needed her out front.

About eleven, Roberta came to the back wearing a twisted grin that seemed to say, *You foxy girl! You fooled me! Not sure I care for that!*

"Some man is here to see you."

Ellen followed her to the sales floor. Will was standing inside the entry door. His hair had been blown about, and he was patting at it with a hand. He was backlit and seemed to glow. It was as if the golden chariot he'd descended on was parked right outside the door. He was tanned and heavier, arms and shoulders bigger from his work, wearing work boots and khaki pants and a white collared shirt that set off this sun-hued skin. She caught her breath, felt tugged toward him like an inner tidal surge and had to stop herself from drifting like a sleepwalker right into an embrace.

They smiled at each other in a tortured, nervous way.

"I'm here."

She longed to hug him and be hugged, but Roberta was apparently determined to witness their reunion. While her spirit soared to meet her Skinny Boy, her body was locked in place. His expression told her he took that to be a lack of enthusiasm.

"You must be the friend. I'm Roberta." She stepped forward to extend her hand, and Will—apparently with great relief—grabbed it with an overblown bonhomie.

"Oh, hi! Roberta! I'm Will. Gee, it's really nice to meet you! Ellen told me you made her feel right at home."

"Happy to do it. She's been part of my family. My son's in medical school at Tulane, but he's here off and on to enjoy her company, too."

"We're going to lunch now!" Ellen blurted out. "I'll see you tomorrow."

Ellen grabbed Will by the arm and steered him through the door. She strode briskly, eyes to the walk, mute, tugging him around the corner, where she stopped, flung her arms about his neck, and burst into tears.

"Oh, gee, I am so damned happy to see you!" she finally choked out.

"Gosh! I am so happy you're so happy!" He sounded giddy. They hugged in silence, swaying, as passersby stepped around them.

"Are you really really happy?" she asked.

"Yes! I'm really really happy to see you!"

"I was afraid... Well, never mind. Are you hungry?"

"You bet."

She deliberately led him to the diner where Tim had treated her so often. She couldn't have said why, but she felt people needed to see her with Will.

He ordered a Rueben and a glass of milk and she an egg salad sandwich she doubted she'd eat.

For a while they were like old classmates who'd bumped into each other. He conjured up vignettes about the boarding house denizens, his co-workers, his roommate Frank and his uncle Kirby. He said he and Frank had made a quick trip to Monterrey to see the sights in a foreign country. He'd picked up a little español. *Fruta.* He winked. *"Tu eres una muchacha linda!"*

"What's that mean?"

"You're a very pretty girl. Frank said it to all the *señoritas.*"

"Not sure I'm flattered, then."

She offered up thumbnail sketches of customers—one cranky old thing and another most peculiar fellow—and she skittered around the topic of the Boyds, stressing her connection to Roberta. She longed to ask him, *Why did you stop writing me?*

When a lapse came as he was finishing his apple pie, she asked, "So is everybody okay?"

He looked puzzled.

"The medical emergency."

He looked grave, very serious, a most uncommon expression.

"I've hated to tell you. Didn't want to bother you with it."

"Well, now I *am* worried, silly boy."

"I am sick. Very sick."

After a moment, he grinned. "Love sick. Heart sick. I needed a big dose of Ellen–o–ane. You think I could get it from that doctor your boss talked about?"

She leaned over the table and swatted him with her napkin. "So you didn't even go home? You came directly here?"

He nodded. "Had to sleep on a bench in the station last night in New Orleans."

"Well, I feel honored."

"You know I wouldn't do it for just any old body."

"Good to hear."

They walked to the park where, not long ago, Ellen and Tim had gone after a movie. Ellen led Will right to the same iron bench with flaking green paint. There were mostly old people sunning themselves and young mothers with kids in strollers. It was a tad too warm, and she was glad for the cotton dress. Will's head was dappled with shade, the lenses of his glasses flickering back the light around them.

She scooted so they were hip to hip and arm to arm, and she took one of his hands between her own. She felt comfortable with him again. She might yawn without covering her mouth; they both might fall silent and feel no need to fill it with chatter. Apropos of nothing, she might tell him about a book she was reading, her need for better shoes, the way she missed her grandmother, how annoyingly noisy the Y was.

She leaned into him and laid her cheek on his chest. His heartbeats were at her ear. His smell. She remembered now how it always made her want to crawl inside him. He laid his arm across her back and cupped her shoulder with a palm. Enclosed by his arms, cheek to his chest, it was like feeling deliciously sleepy in a clean warm bed.

"It's nice here."

She pulled upright, not wanting to be a spectacle. He was looking about at the huge trees overhead. "It reminds me of Nashville."

"What's Texas like?"

"The part I'm in has an ocean. You'd like that—it smells a little fishy and moist but it cools you off and the constant sound is pretty darned soothing. Also, this might sound strange, but the weight of it has an effect on you when you walk beside it. I don't know exactly how to say it. Like it's calling out to all your cells, kind of tugging at them."

"I like oceans."

"Palm trees, too. There's a bird there I know you'd like a lot—a crested Caracara. Big and colorful. Kind of like a cross between one of those gussied-up show roosters and a hawk. I know you like trees and birds."

"I do like trees. And birds."

"And oleander bushes, too. All over the place. Really big, with pink and yellow and purple blossoms. I know you love flowers."

"I do love flowers."

"And, sure, the seafood's great—especially shrimp, Gulf shrimp! Mmmm, man! I know you love shrimp."

"I do love shrimp."

"So there's a whole lot to love in Texas."

She met his warm, smiling gaze with her own. All her worries were evaporating. The distance she'd felt and feared, the emotional turmoil and uncertainty, were eroding before a sudden wave of trust in the thing between them, the three that their one and one made. It was if she'd been too cold all spring and hadn't realized it, but when Will showed up, she remembered what it was like to be warm. She realized then he'd soon leave for Texas, and she'd be cold again and too confused. She'd forgotten how being near him pushed everything else in her life to a distant edge. Her heart beat in her temples, and something inside gave way.

She took a deep breath. "I know there must be a whole lot to love in Texas if you're there."

"Oh, mercy!" He laughed, took off his glasses and mimed wiping them. "I gotta make sure I'm seeing straight!" He slipped them on, squinting, moved his face closer to hers. "Yep, it's Ellen, all right!"

She grinned, pushed him playfully away.

"Did you just almost tell me you love me?!"

She laughed, blushing. "I guess I did."

As she might've feared, he took that as a cause for celebration. He leapt up, strutted about, clowning, made a megaphone of hands to mouth and whooped a bit, but he knew her well enough to avoid a scene—he went mute and pantomimed, pointed at her, pointed back at his heart, his lips forming *YOU! ME! US!*

"Oh, shut up!" she said, laughing.

He sat back down. After a moment, he said, in complete earnest, "Okay. I guess we have to decide on the next step."

The immediate next step was to stroll aimlessly about for a few hours, talking. He said he was sorry for having punished her by not writing. "I was sore," he said. "I was acting like a baby."

She said she was sorry again for how she acted Christmas.

They had dinner at a cafe and talked until the kitchen closed, and then he walked her to her YWCA on 20th just before the curfew. Earlier, he'd registered at the men's Y a few blocks away on the same street.

They took advantage of a broken street light bulb to kiss.

"I need you to be someone I can depend on," she said.

"That'll be my favorite job!"

"What do you want from me?"

"Just keep on being your same old knotty self."

"That I can probably do, sadly."

Later, alone in her room, she could no longer avoid writing to Tim. She apologized for not being forthright about her relationship with Will (and didn't try to excuse or rationalize her silence), wrote that she valued their friendship and that she was deeply grateful for how he'd made her feel less lonely. She closed with "I wish you only the best for your future, and I know you'll be a great success," feeling, as she did, that the words were as empty as the boilerplate birthday greeting from an insurance company.

Thursday morning, over breakfast at the Tim/Will diner, she and Will recalled the promises they made the night before, and since they sounded a bit like vows, they decided the next step was to the Jefferson County Courthouse to get a marriage license.

Then, next step was an awkward, tearful goodbye to Roberta, who half-heartedly wished her all the happiness but added, a tad sternly, "You will write to Tim, of course."

"I already have," said Ellen. "I'm sorry, really. I didn't want to hurt him, he's such a good man."

"Oh, he's a big boy," Robert said brusquely. "I'm sure he'll get over you."

A wedding was out of the question. Even though their families might be disappointed not to attend one, they'd also be relieved not to pay for one.

"I think we can do it at the courthouse," said Will. "That's fine with me."

"Really? To my grandmother that would be as meaningful as getting a building permit."

"Okay, so we'll find a preacher. How about a ring? Do you need a ring?"

"Not today. Someday, though. Go get a cigar, one with a really colorful band, and that can be a stand-in."

"You got it."

So the next step was to find that preacher and with luck a church to go with him. A few calls turned up an invitation to come the next morning, Friday, April 9th, at 10 a.m. to the office of The Rev. Ewart M. Wylie at the First Christian Church.

The church was a 20-minute walk from the YWCA.

With a janitor as a witness, the Rev Wylie married them, and by mid-afternoon they were on the train to Texas. *

147

----

*Author's note: I inherited a trove of documents that includes the letter from "Tim," numerous letters from my dad to my mother before they married, and many from that grandmother to her later in their lives. Aside from what I knew from those letters and journals, I had gleaned details about them from years of knowing them and from historical research. From all this I hoped to stage a "reenactment" of this crucial time in their relationship when my mother was poised between two men who desired her and had to choose one over the other. They were married for 63 years.

In her early fifties, my mother bought herself a chartreuse VW Karmann Ghia.

About the Author

C.W. Smith is the author of the novels *Thin Men of Haddam, Country Music, The Vestal Virgin Room, Buffalo Nickel, Hunter's Trap, Gabriel's Eye, Understanding Women, Purple Hearts, Steplings,* and *Girl Flees Circus.* He has also published a collection of short stories (*Letters from the Horse Latitudes*), a collection of essays (*A Throttled Peacock: Observations on the Old World*), and a memoir (*Uncle Dad*).

He has twice won the "best novel" Award from the Texas Institute of Letters, and he has received the Southwestern Library Association Award for Best Novel, as well as Border Regional Library Association Award for Outstanding Book about the Southwest. Other accolades include the Dobie-Paisano Creative Writing Fellowship from the University of Texas, National Endowment for the Arts Creative Writing Fellowships, the Texas Headliner's Feature Story award, the Frank O'Connor Memorial Short Story Award from Quartet magazine, the John H. McGinnis Short Story Award from Southwest Review; a Pushcart Prize Nomination from Southwest Review, and an award for Best Nonfiction Book by a Texan in from the Southwestern Booksellers Association. He is also a recipient of the Lon Tinkle award for lifetime achievement from The Texas Institute of Letters.

Smith lives in Dallas and is a Dedman Family Distinguished Professor (emeritus) at Southern Methodist University.

His website–http://www.cwsmiththeauthor.com
And on Facebook–https://www.facebook.com/CWSmiththeauthor

Author's Note:

Some stories in this collection were previously published, and I'd like to express gratitude to the editors of those publications for putting them into print. "The Museum of Marriage" originally appeared in *Texas Bound III* as "The Bundelays" and was performed before live audiences in Dallas, Houston, and Denver by Tony Award-winning actress Judith Ivey. "Familiar Strangers" appeared in *The Southwest Review* and received a Pushcart Prize nomination. *The Southwest Review* also published "Caustic," which won the Kay Cattarulla Award for Best Short Story from the Texas Institute of Letters in 2010. "Leave Me Be" and "Costume Jewelry" both appeared in *descant*.

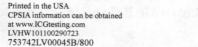

9 781942 956983